ANNIE HARLAND CREEK

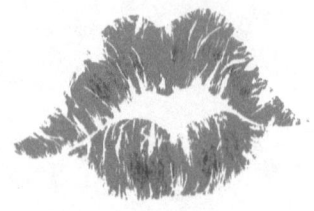

EVERNIGHT PUBLISHING ®

www.evernightpublishing.com

Copyright© 2019

Annie Harland Creek

Editor: CA Clauson

Cover Artist: Jay Aheer

ISBN: 978-1-77339-968-3

ANNIE HARLAND CREEK

DEDICATION

Dedicated to my fellow misfits.

ANNIE HARLAND CREEK

AND NOW YOU'RE MINE

Blood Brothers, 4

Annie Harland Creek

Copyright © 2018

⟨⟨ ·•◆•· ⟩⟩

Prologue

"I sense the presence of an evil spirit," she informs the owners after inspecting the three-story mansion. "This will take a special incantation to exorcise. But, in order to keep the demon from returning, a talisman should be hung…" She scans the room before pointing to the family portrait hanging above the fireplace. "Here! This will protect all who abide in the home."

"How much will that cost?" The husband frowns at his wife.

"I'm not even sure I can expel the spirit. It's very draining." She shakes her head. "Purging spirits takes a toll on me, both spiritually and physically."

Rolling his eyes, the man sighs and turns to his wife. "I told you not to invite a gypsy into our home. She's a charlatan. Next thing, she'll be demanding hundreds of dollars to pay for her medical bills. I bet she took one look at our neighborhood and jacked the price up." He turns back to the gypsy. "Get out of my house, you witch!"

Smash!

Three pairs of eyes stare down at the broken chandelier. Shards of glass and crystal litter the floor. The man brushes some of the debris off his shoulders. His wife's eyes are as big as saucers.

"Come on, Irene. Surely you don't believe a ghost did that? The bulb overheated, that's all."

Crash!

"How do you explain that!" Irene shrieks as she backs away from the broken porcelain vase, ignoring the puddle of water and the oriental lilies strewn over the carpet.

The man scratches his head. "Must have been the wind."

Whack!

Blood gushes from the gash above his eyebrow as he stares down at the bowling trophy that just flew across the room. His face pales and he holds his chest.

"How much?"

"Five hundred dollars."

"That's extortion." He bellows. "I won't –,"

Whoosh!

Flames surge in the unlit fireplace. Irene screams.

"Pay her, Tom. Give her whatever she wants or I'm leaving you and taking the kids to my mother's."

Tom reaches into his jacket pocket and draws out his wallet. "Do you take American Express."

"Cash only." The gypsy tells him with a toothy grin.

Chapter One

Evangeline sat at the small kitchen table in her campervan separating the day's takings into neat piles. Seven hundred dollars. Not bad for a day's work. *Ugh!* She closed her eyes and rubbed her temples with her fingertips. *Damn, these headaches are getting worse.* Blinding light forked behind her eyes. Bile rose in her throat. She took a deep breath and forced herself to her feet. *Can't risk passing out, leaving this money laying around.* It was always a risk parking the van out in secluded bushland, but what choice did she have? Fancy, shmantsy neighborhoods like this one tended to frown upon the intrusion of rusty old vans parking on the pristine streets outside their mansions. Who could blame them? Her home looked as much an oddity as she did.

Pushing her clothes aside, she punched the code into the small security safe hidden inside her wardrobe and placed the money inside. Once secure, she flopped back on her single bed and groaned. *Too bright in here.* With a wave of her hand, she closed all the curtains. *Ah. That's better.*

She adjusted her position on the worn mattress, avoiding the broken springs as she curled into the fetal position. A gust of cold air blew in through the cracked window. She shivered and raised her hand towards the hand-sewn quilt strewn over the only chair in the room. It flew to her, covering her body, but offering little warmth against the chill that had begun to creep into her mobile home. If she'd had the energy, she would have changed out of her gypsy costume and into her warm jeans and hoody, but, for the third night in a row, the headache had left her too exhausted to change. Had she eaten today? Yesterday? She couldn't remember. *Too nauseated to think about food.* Besides, another family had made an appointment for her 'special' services later tonight. They expected Madame Eva, not plain old, Evangeline. Just a couple of hours of sleep and she'd be ready. Ready to create enough havoc to drive up the price she'd quoted. Ready to take these new suckers for as much as she could.

****

Under cover of darkness, Christoff Berg leapt the six-foot brick wall protecting the three- story mansion and walked up the path towards the fast approaching guard dogs.

"Sit!" he commanded them, emphasizing his order with an outstretched hand.

The three Rottweilers dropped to the ground with a whimper and remained in that position on the gravel driveway as he continued up to the verandah. He glanced up at the security camera and smiled, knowing full well his image would not be detected. No camera had ever recorded his image. None ever would.

He shimmered into the home, focusing on the honeyed voice of the thief he'd been tracking for weeks. Once inside, he remained incorporeal, as he watched her perform her act of deception.

"Yes. There is an evil spirit in this house." She told the immaculately dressed occupants. "Possibly two." She closed her eyes and breathed deeply. "I can help you, but it won't be cheap."

"You already quoted us one thousand dollars." The female complained. "That's all I'm prepared to pay."

The gypsy nodded and smiled. "You told me over the phone that you thought you had a ghost. Had I known you had demons, the price would have been higher."

"How high?" The husband asked, raising an eyebrow.

"Well, my price for demon exorcism is two thousand dollars, but –"

"What do you mean, "but"? The price just doubled. One thousand dollars is outrageous. I won't pay a cent more," he told her.

"I understand." The gypsy responded with a smile and flipped her long, unruly hair behind her. Hair as dark as her doe eyes. "I won't waste any more of your time."

The owners led her towards the front door. *Was she leaving without an argument? Without a sales pitch? What is she playing at?*

"Daddy!"

The parents ran upstairs, the father taking the steps two at a time while the child's screams reverberated throughout the house. Christoff shimmered ahead of them and waited inside the child's room. The little girl sat curled into a ball on her bed, clutching her teddy bear and screaming at the top of her lungs. The bed floated three feet off the ground.

"Holy mother of god," the father shouted as he entered the room.

"My baby!" the child's mother screamed as she rushed to the little girl.

The gypsy extended both her arms. "I command you to put down the child."

Instantly, the bed crashed to the ground and the mother snatched her sobbing daughter and ran from the room.

"This is worse than I thought," the raven-haired beauty informed them with a shake of her head.

A low growl escaped from Christoff's lips and he clenched his teeth. There were no demons present in this room. He was sure of it. She alone caused the bed to rise. *She* terrified the child in order to extort money from the parents. *What type of monster uses a toddler like that?*

Undetected, he followed them from the room and down two flights of stairs, profiling the woman who had perfected the art of deception. Her stereotypically gypsy attire worked well for her and the off the shoulder, embroidered peasant blouse revealed more than a little cleavage. A black leather belt cinched her at the waist, accentuating her voluptuous body. This woman would never walk the fashion runways with the stick skinny models. The curve of her ample buttocks was not quite Rubenesque, more Jayne Mansfield. This was a body made for sex.

"I definitely believe there are two demons at work here." She grasped the man's hands. "We must work quickly before they—"

"Before they what?" the man gasped. "Do they plan on hurting my baby?"

"I must warn you. I've dealt with these things many times. They may try to possess her. I'll need to make protection amulets for all of you, get supplies, prepare myself mentally for the ordeal. I'll be back tomorrow night to perform the ritual."

"You can't leave us!" They turned towards the mother who stood in the doorway clutching tightly to the sobbing child. "Please. Do something!"

"I will." The gypsy told her. "But not tonight. You must take your little one and stay in a hotel tonight. Go pack a bag."

When the mother ran up the stairs to pack, she turned to the father, grabbing him by the bicep. "Tomorrow, come alone. Things may get violent. I don't want to risk the child again."

Ah. Thinking of the child. Maybe she does have a little compassion. His opinion changed when she finished giving her instructions.

"Bring three thousand dollars. I only accept cash."

****

"Too easy." The gypsy mumbled under her breath as she waved a solemn farewell to the anxious family and headed back to her mobile home on foot. Once out of sight, she let loose a little squeal of delight. *Easy money. Once I get that father alone, I'll pull out the big guns.* She cupped her breasts, pushing them up to the point where they almost spilled from her shirt. *Works like a charm.* Charm? *Damn.* She'd promised a protective amulet for each member of the household. Each home-made medallion took twenty-four hours to set. *Fuck.* She slipped her hand into her pocket and retrieved her mobile phone, rolling her eyes as she dialed the dreaded number.

"Well, hi there, sweet cheeks. Got any new merchandise? Of course, I'm willing to trade, *if* the charms look authentic." A shiver ran through her body and she almost gagged. Next time she'd make sure she had enough supplies.

****

"Evangeline. Always a pleasure." Wheezed the overweight pawn shop owner as she sashayed into his store. "I have something special for you."

"I'm sure you have." She leaned over to examine the drawer full of tarnished knick knacks. As if on cue, the front of her blouse gaped, revealing black lace and plump skin.

His eyes widened, cheeks flushed, and a dribble of saliva ran down his chin. *Charming.*

"Eyes up here, Neville." She told him with a smile. "Let's see if you have anything worth trading first."

"I'm sure you'll find something you like." He promised. His voice bubbled with enthusiasm. "I found some really special designs for you." His index finger tugged at his shirt collar. The bulge in his pants quivered.

"Maybe this time we could—"

She shook her head. "You know the deal." With a shrug, she added, "If you're not satisfied with our arrangement, I *could* take my business elsewhere."

"No. The usual deal will be fine." He wiped at his sweaty forehead with a filthy handkerchief before stuffing it back into his pocket. "Three charms for—"

"Four charms," she corrected with a wag of her finger. "I hope you're not trying to cheat poor little ol' me, Neville."

"But I thought … never mind." His cheeks turned the color of a stop light as he hurried to lock the front door. "Shall we retire to the back room?"

"Whatever you want," she agreed, swallowing the acrid taste of bile in her mouth. "Oops, slip of the tongue." She ran a lazy tongue over her top lip. He groaned and clutched at his crotch as he ushered her behind the beaded curtain that concealed his bedroom. *Thank god.* She sighed. *Looks like this will be over quick.*

****

"Yes! That's it. That's what I want," he groaned between his grimy, faded bed sheets.

"How about this?"

"Oh, yes. Please. That too. Take that off."

She closed her eyes as the lacy bra landed beside her discarded shirt on the filthy floor. *Yuck. I think I'll need to burn these things when I get home.*

"Please, let me touch them." He cried out as his hand jerked beneath the sheets.

"You know the rules," she scolded. "Look, don't touch."

"You're killing me, Evangeline." He groaned. "At least let me see *you* touch them."

Bringing her index fingers to her lips, she drew the digits into her mouth and sucked, in and out, again and again, before placing them to her breasts. Moistening her nipples with her own saliva as she drew lazy circles around her areola, she tried to imagine herself somewhere else. Anywhere else. Thankfully, as her fingers brushed inside the waistband of her cut-off shorts, he climaxed. *There is a god.*

"Just relax," she told him as she retrieved her clothes from the bedroom floor, fastened her bra, and threw on her shirt, "I'll just grab my five charms and head off."

"Four charms," he called after her as she raced from the room with her blouse unbuttoned.

"Are you sure?"

"I think … no, I'm sure we agreed on four. Hang on, I'll come out and show you the prettiest baubles. The ones worthy of you."

Pockets bulging, she hurried to the door. "Don't worry, Neville. We both got what we deserved."

****

The cut off shorts hit the floor of the campervan with a thud as she hurried to the tiny shower recess, stripping off completely before she reached the door. As the hot water began streaming down on her bare skin, she reached outside the cubicle and grabbed her bra and shirt. *No point wasting water.* Scented shampoo bubbles ran down her body and pooled at her feet. She used her foot to agitate the clothes against the tiles as a shudder shook her body. If only she could wash away the memories along with the dirt.

Wrapping her body in a terry cloth robe and a towel around her thick, damp hair, she retrieved her shorts and emptied the contents of her pockets onto the small kitchen table. A smile curled one side of her mouth as she sifted through the pile of golden trinkets. *Nice haul.* Fifteen, no, at least twenty items. She chose three, but, as she brushed the others aside for later use, she yelped. *Fuck. That hurt.* A red welt began to form and blister on her palm. Hesitantly, she touched the pile. Cold. How could a stack of cold trinkets produce an instant burn?

Jumping at the alarm on her phone, she soon forgot about the burn as she hurried to dress for her appointment, paying special attention to her makeup and clothes. If he acted on her instructions, the husband would be there alone. A lamb to the slaughter. One way or another, she'd get more money from him. *Him* with his huge house and expensive cars. He'd hardly miss a couple of thousand. Maybe she could even squeeze ten? Pocketing the three charms, she locked the door to her rundown home. *Soon*, she promised herself. *Soon, I'll leave this life behind.*

Chapter Two

Christoff sat perched in the overhanging branch of an oak tree and watched the man who paced the porch of the mansion. The gypsy had done her job well, convincing the husband that the lives of his family were in danger from a force inside the home. His anxious glances towards the window betrayed his fear. There was no way he would enter the house alone.

Movement at the gate caught his eye. *Her.* She casually made her way up the long, pebbled drive, either oblivious or possibly uncaring of the man's distress. *This one is a real piece of work.* As she came closer into view, his gaze ran over her body, from her luscious curls to her shapely ankles. Her attire left little to the imagination and clung to her body like a second skin. No man, living or undead, could call himself male and not be tempted by her tantalizing curves. Even his own body betrayed him, hardening in appreciation of the most perfect female specimen he'd seen in many, many years. He forced the emotion away. *Not this woman. This trollop.* She'd set the scene for a seduction. Arranged to meet with the husband alone. She was nothing more than a whore.

She greeted the husband with a handshake, sustaining the grip a little longer than the conventional amount of time. Before releasing it, she stroked his hand, sandwiching it between hers as she told him she wouldn't leave until he was completely satisfied.

"I'm sure you won't." Christoff growled under his breath as he followed them into the house.

"First things first." She slipped a chain around the husband's neck and shook her head. "This won't do." Her lips pouted, forming the shape of a plump, red bow. "Let's get rid of this tie and loosen your collar." She tossed the tie onto the settee and unbuttoned the shirt to his sternum before he could stutter his protest. A brassy looking charm hung half-way down his chest.

"I came straight home from work."

"Well, you must try and relax," she told him with a sly smile, as she slipped her hand inside his shirt, tracing circles on his bare chest. "Evil feeds on fear. We must convince it that we are in control." She lowered her chin, gazed up at him from under a fringe of thick, black lashes. "If the spirits see weakness in you, they may try and control you."

The man's complexion paled. "Control me? How?"

"Let's put negative thoughts out of our minds." She turned her back on him, but Christoff watched her lips curl into a smile. "Let me think. Where would be the best place to start?" She spun around, the smile gone from her devious face. "Show me to the bedrooms."

As they climbed the stairs, she asked the man his Christian name.

"Anthony." He answered automatically. His gaze directed at the room at the top of the stairs.

"Anthony," she repeated, melodically. "Such a strong name."

"I was named after my father and his father before him." Anthony informed her as he stopped in front of his daughter's room.

The gypsy's eye's twinkled. "So, I guess that makes you Anthony Addams the third?"

Christoff's supernatural hearing detected her whispered, "Ca-ching", as she stepped into the child's room to begin her deception. "Do you mind if I call you, Tony."

"Actually, yes. I'd prefer –"

"Hush." With her finger pressed to her lips, she

silenced him. "I need you to remain quiet while I try to detect the entities in the room." She closed her eyes, expanding her chest and holding out her hands as if to welcome a lover into her deadly embrace. "Are there any spirits present?"

A gust of wind blew the curtains and the small crystal chandelier swung from side to side. Christoff shook his head. *Parlor tricks.* Nevertheless, he couldn't help but be a little impressed. She had talent. Talent for knowing the best use of her powers, and talent for choosing the right victims. A chandelier in a child's bedroom? These people had more money than sense.

She opened her eyes, turning towards Anthony as she told him. "They are angry with us for being here. I feel their hatred towards me." With an open hand, she fanned her face. "Is it getting hot in here? I'm feeling a little…" Her legs buckled beneath her, but with plenty of time for her prey to catch her before she fell.

Clever girl.

After positioning her on the end of the child's bed, Anthony rushed to the ensuite and returned with a wet compress.

"Thank you," she sighed, moistening her forehead and cheeks with the compress. She kept her eyes trained on his face as she lowered the cloth to her neck, then chest, pausing for effect at her cleavage.

When she unfastened the first few buttons of her blouse to pat at the skin of her breasts, the husband's eyes widened. As did Christoff's. Despite their size, her plump, tanned breasts almost defied gravity. His fingers twitched as he imagined squeezing the tender orbs. Anthony, gasped and turned away.

The gypsy may not have seen the bulge in the distinguished, Anthony Addams the third's tailored trousers, but the twinkle in her eye provided Christoff with the information he suspected. More of her parlor tricks. As he adjusted the crotch of his own pants, he wondered, *just how far would this woman go?*

"I'm feeling a little better now." She rose from the bed and dipped into the pocket of her skirt. "Take this charm for your wife. I'll place the other on the dresser for your lovely daughter." As she moved towards the dresser, her skirt blew up over her head, fluttering there long enough to allow both men an enjoyable view of her ample derriere. *What type of undergarment is this?* Christoff could hardly believe she would find the garment comfortable. The thin scrap of silk not much more than a band at her waist, completely exposing her buttocks. What was the point of even wearing such a thing? She turned, her skirt still flapping around her ears and he gasped. A triangle of almost transparent white lace, accentuating rather than covering her private parts. *White?* Was she playing the ingénue? He suspected her innocence had been taken long ago.

"Oh, my," she squealed, forcing the skirt to behave. "They seem to be annoyed at me for helping you. I'm so embarrassed." Her hands shot to her cheeks and her chin lowered.

After clearing his voice, Anthony assured her she had nothing to be ashamed about. The color in his cheeks told a different story, as did the bulge in his pants. Something inside Christoff stirred. Something buried deep down for centuries. A low growl resonated through the room. The gypsy's eyes widened, and she turned her head quickly from side to side. Had she heard him? She shook her head. A subtle shake but there, nonetheless. He'd need to be more careful. He wasn't ready to confront her, not yet. Not until he'd learned as much as he could.

She moved towards the man with the agility of a

jungle cat and reached up to grasp the charm at his sternum. "We must work quickly, using our collective energies. I will focus on the power of your charm while you hold tight to the one around my neck."

The elegant Mr. Addams the third, gulped as he reached inside the gypsy's shirt, fumbling at her breasts as he drew on the deceptively long chain. By the time he'd located the charm, his cheeks were as red as the tie he'd discarded in the living room, and her blouse gaped even wider. She leaned into him, mumbling a chant as she pushed her breasts against the charm, forcing his hands deep into her blouse. Forcing her hips against his growing erection.

How far did she plan to take this sham? Would she really sell her body? *Of course, she would, you fool.* She'd already extorted thousands from this family and that was *before* she'd established his worth. He leaned back against a wall and waited for her next move. He didn't have to wait long.

Suddenly, she flew backwards onto the bed, her skirt once again around her ears. Christoff blinked, then blinked again. Had his eyes deceived him? Did the husband push her?

"What are you doing?" she screamed at the man who fumbled at his zipper as he approached the bed.

"I don't know!" he yelled back. "Honestly, I don't understand what's happening."

Despite his denial, Anthony maneuvered himself between her legs, tearing her blouse open, cupping her breasts, all the while protesting his innocence. She wiggled beneath him, begging him to stop. Pleading with him. It was almost convincing. *Almost.*

Anger boiled in Christoff's belly. Instinct told him to aim his fury at the charlatan, certain she had choreographed the entire situation. *She* was the puppet master. Despite this, he found himself desperate to annihilate the puppet. Wanting to tear him limb from limb. How dare he touch those breasts? Pathetic human with pathetic human lusts. Surely his love for his wife would have given him the strength to fight her seduction? Has he no willpower at all? No self-respect?

With a shove, she managed to push him away before the situation intensified.

"I'm so sorry." Anthony sobbed as he backed away from the bed, zipping his fly. "It must have been the spirits controlling me."

She sat up, flattening down her skirt as her breasts jiggled free of the cotton blouse, tempting Christoff to test the weight for himself. She took her time covering her modesty, tying the ends of her torn blouse in a knot before slipping her feet over the edge of the bed.

"This has never happened to me before." She informed him, a tremble in her voice. "I think I should speak to your wife about it. Ask if you've ever done something like this to another woman. If she verifies your story, I won't press charges."

"My wife? No. Please don't tell my wife." He begged, cupping his hands in front of his chest. "She wouldn't understand."

She rose to her feet and tidied up the mass of curls with her fingers as she pretended to wipe a tear from her eye. "I don't know you or your wife, Mr. Addams but I can't let this sort of behavior go unpunished. You tried to –"

"Please, Madame Eva. I'm begging you. I love my wife. I've never cheated on her." He dropped to his knees on the floor. Christoff almost felt sorry for the man as he begged for absolution.

"I'll pay you extra to forget this happened." Fumbling into his pants' pocket, he pulled out a wad of bills and counted out four thousand dollars. "Here." He pushed the money at the not-so-distressed woman. "An extra thousand to forget this ever happened?"

She snatched the money from his hand and glared down at him. "Four thousand? You think my silence can be bought with a measly one thousand dollars?"

"But –"

"Must I remind you, Tony. You had your sweaty palms on my boobs, squeezing them for all they're worth." She simulated her accusations using her own cupped hands for effect. "You had your pecker almost inside me. If I hadn't pushed you, who knows how far you'd have gone."

He dropped down, sitting on his heels. His hands covering his face as he sobbed.

"I know, I know. Something compelled me to do it. I couldn't control myself. I wanted you so badly, I would have … oh, god. I'm so sorry."

"I believe that you're sorry." She told him with a condescending pat to his head. "But I'm going to need lots of therapy to get over this. Lots of *expensive* therapy."

"Take it all." He emptied his pockets, spilling hundred dollar bills at her feet. "Just, please. Don't tell anyone what happened. It would be the ruin of me."

She leaned down, scooped the notes into her pocket and strolled to the door, calling over her shoulder as she left. "The evil presence has left the room. I will cast it completely from the house on my way out."

Christoff shimmered after her as she made her way down the stairs and out of the house. For the first time that night, she had told the truth. Evil had indeed left the house, and, if he had anything to do with it, she wouldn't be back.

Chapter Three

After a quick stop at the liquor store, Evangeline hurried back to her mobile home. The weight in her skirt pocket reminded her to hurry. Nothing good could come of wandering the streets alone at night, especially carrying thousands of dollars in cash. The occasional footstep behind her made her turn. No one. She reasoned that her imagination was playing tricks but rushed anyway. She'd worked hard for that money and no one was going to take that away. Not again.

Her hands shook as she turned the key and she almost dropped it. *What's wrong with you?* Once inside, she locked the three deadlocks and plonked down on the bed. Safe. Well, as safe as one could be in a broken down, crap-heap of a campervan. She pulled the notes from her pocket, spreading them over the worn quilt. So many hundred-dollar bills. A squeal of delight escaped unbidden. She covered her mouth with her hand. The area she'd chosen to park the van may have been isolated, but you never knew who might be within earshot.

After stacking the notes in piles of ten, she began counting her stash. One, two, three, four, five. *Five thousand dollars!* She gave herself a mental pat on the back. Not bad for one night's work. But, as usual, the exhilaration soon dissipated when she thought back to how she'd acquired the windfall. *Poor Tony.* He seemed like a nice guy. Most of her targets *were* nice people. Nice, *rich*, people. People who could easily manage with a few thousand less in their fat bank accounts. The familiar pang of guilt tied knots in her stomach, she doubled over and groaned, trying to convince herself that she was merely hungry. The pain passed. The guilt didn't.

She grabbed the brown paper bag from the bed,

grateful that she'd remembered to make a pit-stop on the way home. *It's just you and me again, Jim.* The bottle declined to answer, but she didn't mind. The sweet, dark liquid may not have been much of a conversationalist, but it was good company on a lonely, summer's eve. Evangeline sighed. *What would Mama think if she could see me, sitting alone, drinking from a bottle?* Tears burned behind her eyes, but she blinked them away and reached for her cell phone.

"Hello, Mama?"

"Evangeline? Is that you, baby?"

"Yes, Mama. How are you? Are they treating you well?"

"I'm fine, honey. Just fine. Excuse me a minute..." Cough. "The staff here are very kind, but I miss you. When are you coming to visit me?"

"Soon." She stared down at the piles of cash. "My boss just gave me a bonus. Soon I'll have enough money for a deposit on a small house. We can be together again."

"I'd like that." Her mother said. "I'd like that very much, but—"

"I know what you're going to say, and I don't want to hear it." Evangeline covered her mouth with her hand, swallowing the sob that threatened to betray her. Must stay strong for Mama. "You're going to get well."

After a long pause, her mother spoke.

"I know you're very busy at work, but I'd really like to see you. There are things I need to say, things you should know. Important things."

"Next week. I could be there by Friday. Would that be okay?" *Will that be too late?*

"Friday! Oh, darling. That would be wonderful. I can't wait to see you."

"Then, it's a date. I gotta go now. Sweet dreams."

"Sweet dreams, my darling. Mwah. I love you so much."

"I love you, too."

She depressed the "hang up" key and dissolved into tears. *Hang on Mama. I'll get the money, somehow. We'll find a cure.* The pile of money seemed to shrink before her eyes. Not enough. Not nearly enough for both a deposit on a home plus medical expenses. Together with the bag of money stashed in the wall safe, she had a grand total of seventy-eight thousand dollars.

Gotta think. She took another swig from the bottle before hiding the night's takings with the rest of her money. Mama sounded dreadful. Worse than the last time they spoke. How much time did she have left? She stalked the tiny home, taking large gulps of alcohol from the bottle as she thought aloud.

"I need to pull off something big. Something worth hundreds of thousands. But how?"

The lights in the room began to flicker in quick succession.

"Damned generator!" Slamming the bourbon down onto the table, she opened the kitchen cabinet and snatched up three candles and a packet of matches. Before she had time to light them, the lights went out.

"Fuck."

Black as pitch, the inside of the home seemed darker than outside. She opened the curtains a little to allow the moon to illuminate the room. No sooner had she done so, when she noticed it. Something on the table emitted its own light. On closer inspection, she gasped. Slap dang in the middle of the pile of trinkets, glowed one particularly unusual medallion. Hesitantly, she reached out and touched the object with the tip of her index finger, immediately regretting her decision.

"Ouch!"

She fumbled her way to the sink and held her finger to the cold water until the pain subsided, but the damage was already done. *Damn. That's going to blister.* Intuition warned her to destroy the object or, at the very least, toss it far into the woods, but she fought the impulse. Whatever this was, it had power. Heaps of it. If she could somehow learn to harness this power…

"What the fuck?"

A face stared back at her through the window. A male face, as pale as snow with eyes as cold as a blizzard. *The money!* As she ran to the kitchen, her thoughts raced to the small wall safe. *How much had he seen?* She snatched up the largest knife she could find and turned back to the window. The gall of the man. He hadn't moved, despite knowing he'd been noticed. What nerve.

"I have a knife and I'm prepared to use it," she warned as the knife shook in her hand.

His expression remained unchanged, unaffected by her threat. Ice cold. She considered jumping into the driver's seat and driving away, but as if he could read her mind, he shook his head. Bile rose in her throat. She swallowed it down, regretting the large quantity of alcohol she'd consumed. *Think, Evangeline.*

"Give me the medallion." He ordered. A pane of glass the only thing between her and the intruder. She shook her head and used the knife blade to slide the medallion into her pocket. If this man wanted it so bad, it must be worth a fortune.

"Go fuck yourself." She told him, embarrassed at how meek the words sounded aloud. She'd hoped to sound intimidating. She didn't.

"Give me the medallion, and I'll let you live."

Let me live? Her heart beat a mile a minute and she found breathing difficult. She leaned against the kitchen table for support as the strength left her legs.

God, help me. He's gonna kill me. She fixed her gaze on the man, afraid to look, afraid to look away. Nothing in his expression gave her any hope of convincing him to spare her. Despite his handsome features, the long straight nose, the cropped wheat-blond hair and ice-blue eyes, there was no doubt in her mind. This man was a stone-cold killer.

"Open the door." He instructed, and her legs obeyed.

What? No! She forced herself to stop just as her hand touched the first lock. What the hell? How was he doing that?

"Open the door!" he repeated as she fought the compulsion to comply.

"I don't know how you're doing that, but stay the fuck out of my head, you asshole!"

She turned back to face the window. His expression had changed slightly. He seemed more focused, maybe a little annoyed.

"You *will* let me in."

"No, I won't." *At least I hope I won't.* The compulsion intensified as she stared into his hypnotic, pale eyes. Must fight it. Mustn't look into his eyes.

She reached out, grabbing the edges of the curtains, and pulled them shut. It was a risk, she knew that, but what choice did she have? Somehow, he had found a way to use his eyes to control her mind. Another thought hit her. A realization that gave her hope of surviving the night. The supernatural abilities. The pale skin and hypnotic eyes. She'd heard stories of creatures with those characteristics but, until now, she'd never believed them. Vampire.

He can't come in unless invited.

"Open the door!"

The sound of footsteps moved from the side to the

front of the van, stopping outside the door.

She held her breath. Maybe she was wrong. Maybe he was playing a sick game. Maybe this *was* the end. The van shook as he pounded on the door. She covered her ears with her hands and curled into a tight ball on the floor.

"Go away!"

The pounding at the door stopped, but the pounding in her chest increased.

"This isn't over," he warned her. "I'll be watching you."

Minutes turned to hours. Still, she remained on the floor … waiting. Had he really gone? Would he come back tonight? Light began to filter through the gap under the curtains. She rose to her feet, grimacing in pain as she rubbed circulation back into her aching muscles. This day was sure to come. She'd known there'd be a price for her misusing her gift. A day of reckoning. She shook her head. *You've made your bed, now lie in it.* The avenging angel has come to collect. No. Strike that. No angel, not even a man. Her punishment would come at the hands of a vampire.

****

Christoff lay on the bed in his darkened room of the guest house and waited for the sun to go down. His cell phone danced across the bedside table for the third time this morning and, once again, he ignored it, knowing it would be his hosts wanting details about the case. *My case.* When would they get that through their thick skulls? If Lupescu had somehow managed to survive, disposing of the mage was his responsibility and his alone. He neither required, nor desired assistance.

The events of the previous night troubled him. This woman, this charlatan. How had she been able to resist his compulsions? He crossed his arms behind his head and recalled the turn of events. She'd begun to succumb, he'd watched her hand go to the lock and yet … somehow, she'd denied him entry. Puzzling. He tried to recall another time his mind control had failed, and when the memory came to him, it turned his blood to ice. *Lupescu*.

He swung his long legs over the edge of the bed and sprung to his feet, pacing with no idea which direction to follow, until he stalked past the flyer on his desk.

Have you been troubled by unexplained events in your home?

Do your animals react to noises undetectable to the human ear?

Have you noticed cold patches or feeling of foreboding?

Madame Eva is the answer to your problems. Call the number below for an obligation-free quote.

Madame Eva. Hah. If that was her real name. There must be a way to trap her. His cell rang again and, deep in thought, he unwittingly answered it.

"What?"

"Hello to you too, Berg."

"What is it, Palmer? I'm extremely busy."

"Look, it's not my idea to call. Susie was worried about you. You haven't answered her calls."

Christoff felt some of the tension release from his shoulders. *So, the little one worries about me.* He cleared his throat and growled into the phone. "Well, if she's that concerned, why didn't *she* call?"

"Sudden attack of nausea. She's throwing up as we speak, poor kid."

The tension in his neck returned. "Is she ill?"

"Well … she'd planned on telling your herself, but … we're moving up the wedding to next month and she refused to go ahead without you."

"Why the hurry? How ill is she? Wait, you're telling me that she's having a baby?"

"And we couldn't be more pleased, except for the morning sickness that, incidentally, lasts most of the day."

Christoff plonked down on the edge of the bed, the leaflet fluttering to the floor.

"Congratulations." They were a fine couple who deserved nothing less than the joy of a baby. A joy he would never personally experience. "Your happy home will be complete."

He reached down to retrieve the flyer and stopped. *This might work.*

"Palmer. It pains me to ask you, but how would you like to help me catch a thief?"

****

Evangeline checked the address on her cell. No, this was the right place. Bummer. The man on the phone had promised he'd pay anything for her help. Anything. Judging by the look of this house, she'd be lucky to make a couple of hundred. She shrugged her shoulders and marched herself up the pebbled path. *Oh, well. I'm here. I may as well get this over with.*

As she waited for someone to answer her knock, she realized an important issue. *I didn't work my magic on this place.* There may be a real spirit here. She suppressed a giggle. Yeah, whatever. Probably the fertile imagination of a neurotic little man. Raising her arm, she realized she'd forgotten to wear her watch. Whatever. A few flying objects, a sudden gust of wind or two, a theatrical performance and she'd be out in around two hours. Plenty of time to leave town before the vampire returned.

"Hello. You must be Madame Eva."

The handsome young man greeted her with an extended hand which she readily grabbed and held tight.

"Well, hello, yourself." *Maybe I could spare an extra hour or two.* She glanced down at her blouse. *Damn. Why did I wear my favorite? Oh, well. What's another ripped blouse? Que sera, sera.* "Mr. Palmer, I presume."

"Call me Terry," he told her as she entered the home.

"Lovely home you have here, Terry," she told him, trying to act impressed as she looked around the darkened room. The block-out curtains had been pulled closed. Inexpensive lamps illuminated the room.

Sure, it was a lovely home, but not what she'd expected. A couple of extra floors and perhaps a chandelier or two may have given her hope. This was a hundred-dollar job. Nothing more, nothing less. Ah, well. Best get to work.

"You were right to call me here, Terry. I sense a dark presence in this house." With a subtle flick of her wrist, she sent a vase sailing across the room. It hit the wall beside the hallway, just as a pretty young woman stepped into view. The woman ducked in time, rising while holding her stomach.

"Are you okay, honey?" Terry rushed to her side. "I told you to stay in bed."

"I can't spend the entire pregnancy in bed." She scowled. "Besides, I had to use the bathroom, again."

Pregnancy? The contents of Evangeline's stomach churned. No way was she going to risk harming a pregnant woman or her baby.

"I think I've made a mistake." She told them with a shake of her head as she backed towards the door. "There's no danger here."

"Are you sure about that?"

"You!"

Evangeline made a dash for the door. Too late. The vampire blocked her path, his shoulders filling the entire door frame. But how? She glanced past him at the window. The curtains blocked any sunlight that might have filtered through. She turned to run, but found her path blocked by the homeowners.

"I see you've met Christoff?" the young woman asked.

"Not officially." Evangeline turned back towards the vampire. "So, the monster has a name."

Christoff took a step closer, his glacial eyes boring into hers. "You dare to call me a monster?" His top lip curled. "I've seen you exploit children in order to swindle their parents, but what kind of fiend would harm an unborn child for the monetary gain?"

"I would never!" she screamed back at him before turning towards the other woman. "Honestly, I didn't know. I would never have come had I known."

"Liar!" Christoff snarled as he closed the gap between them. "I should end your sorry existence—"

"Woah, Lurch." Terry stepped between them, holding the giant back with his outstretched arms. "She's human. You can't hurt her or else the coven will come down on you like a ton of bricks."

The woman tried a different approach, stroking Christoff's arm as she assured him, "I'm all right. She didn't hurt me, or the baby."

"But—"

"I believe her. She seemed genuinely upset that she'd thrown the vase." She turned to Evangeline who nodded vehemently. "There, see. Now let's all sit down and...oh, no."

"Is she okay?" Evangeline asked as the woman dashed from the room holding her hand over her mouth.

"Morning sickness," Terry informed her. "She'll be gone for a while."

"It's time for me to go, too." She scooted around him, only to be grabbed by the arm. "Let. Me. Go. You. Oaf." Turning back to Terry, she growled. "Can't you control your pet?"

"Our business isn't finished." Christoff informed her as he dragged her over to the settee and forced her to sit.

"You can't keep me here," she warned. "If you fuckin' touch me, I'll scream the place down and your neighbors will call the cops."

"I thought part of your charade was enticing your victims to touch you." Christoff scoffed. "But, rest assured, I have no desire to do so. Even vampires have standards to uphold."

"Ooh, burn!" Terry slapped his thigh and let out a laugh. "I didn't know you had a sense of humor." He was still smiling when he turned to Evangeline and, with a wink, informed her, "And, honey, I *am* the cops."

"Oh, shit!" She leaned back against the settee, crossing her arms as she scowled. "So, what now?"

"Now, you will hand over the medallion." Christoff extended his hand, palm up.

"Fuck off!" *If he wants it so bad, it must be worth a fortune.*

Terry shook his head. "That's not very ladylike, language."

"This one is no lady."

With a forced smile, she raised her middle finger and screwed up her nose. "Listen, you can't prove that I've done anything wrong here. I haven't asked for money, so you can't charge me with anything."

"That's true," Terry scratched his chin, "but our friend here says you've been a naughty girl and, from what he's told me, I imagine there are a few families in Azure Waters who can back up his stories."

"Look. I'm leaving town anyway." She edged forward on the couch. "Just let me go and I promise you'll never hear from me again."

As she tried to rise from her seat, Christoff extended his arm and forced her down, his hand brushing her chest. A shock of electricity tingled her senses, surprising her. Was it anger? Arousal? Whatever it was, she wasn't about to let him know how much she enjoyed the touch of his hand on her breast.

"Did you enjoy that, Chris? Cop a nice feel?"

The giant of a man growled. "My name is Christoff. Christoff Berg."

"Yeah, whatever." She turned her attention back to the other man and smiled her most seductive grin. *Come on charm, don't let me down.* "So, Terry. Do we have a deal?"

The men exchanged glances. Christoff shook his head. Anger rocked her body. *What does he want from me?*

"You asshole!" Jumping to her feet before he could stop her, she slapped his cheek. Hard. Pain shot through her hand and the skin turned red, but he showed no reaction to her attack. "What do you want from me?"

"I want the medallion."

"Well, I don't have it on me." She told him, grateful that she'd left it in her mobile home.

"I don't believe you."

"Then, I'll have to prove it to you."

She grabbed the hem of her blouse and yanked it over her head before stepping out of the skirt. Terry's eyes widened before he turned away. Christoff's face remained expressionless as he picked up the discarded items and shook them.

She posed in her underwear, feet apart and hands on hips as he tossed the clothes onto the settee. She waited for the lude remarks that usually followed her stripteases. The squirmy sensation on her skin and inside her belly that ensued as she tried to ignore the arousals of her targets. Instead, the palms of her own hands became clammy and doubt clouded her thoughts. *Doesn't he find me attractive? Why do I even care?*

"Satisfied?"

"No. You may have the medallion concealed."

"Wait a minute, Lurch. I think you're taking things a bit far." Terry argued as his cheeks flushed.

"Don't worry, Terry," she told him, "he wouldn't dare."

"Oh, wouldn't I?"

Christoff closed the gap, his cold eyes flaring as his gaze drifted down from her face, hovering over her breasts before resting on the lace of her panties. His mouth opened slightly as his tongue swiped over his top lip. Her heart skipped a beat. Would he rip the lace from her body, leaving her naked and vulnerable to his advances? How would he react to the dampness of her thong? His right hand reached out, painfully slowly as he scrutinized the junction of her thighs. She closed her eyes, waiting, imagining his fingers brushing against her arousal. Hating herself for allowing him to have that effect on her body. Wishing he'd hurry.

"Christoff!"

Susie stood in the doorway with her hands on her hips. Pink blotches formed on her pale cheeks as she frowned. "Don't you dare!"

His shoulders dropped, and he stepped away, but not in time to cover the bulge in his expensive jeans. "I must retrieve the medallion."

Susie let out a long sigh and shook her head

before disappearing into another room. When she returned, she sighed. "Men." She turned towards Evangeline, rolling her eyes as she walked towards her, robe in hand. "If there'd been a medallion in her underwear, I'm sure we'd have been able to see it." She motioned to the transparent lace and Evangeline inwardly smiled. The underwear had been specifically purchased to reveal as much skin as possible. It always worked like a charm. The suckers usually shot their load without her ever having to do anything more than wiggle suggestively. Usually. As she slipped into the black silk robe, she wondered how far the vampire would have gone to satisfy his suspicion. What troubled her most was … how far did she *want* him to go?

"How do I look?" She turned around slowly, stalling for time. Think, Evangeline. How are you going to get yourself out of this?

"The color suits you." He scoffed before turning his back to her. "Black like your soulless eyes."

"At least I have a soul." She considered throwing something at his head, then changed her mind. No point in antagonizing him further.

"Look, lady." She appealed to the wife. "As I've explained to Chris and your husband, I don't have this medallion they're talking about. I just want to go back to my campervan and get the hell out of this godforsaken town."

The woman extended her hand. "Susie. My name's Susie. Terry and I aren't married yet. We're making it official next month." While still holding Evangeline's hand, she leaned in and whispered, "You really shouldn't call him Chris. He has a very short fuse."

"Noted." She answered, knowing full well she'd use the information to push his buttons. But not here. Not now, when her actions may hurt the quirky little pregnant woman or the baby growing in her belly. Despite what the vampire had said, she had a soul *and* a heart for that matter. Not that she'd used it for a while.

"Get dressed!" The vampire suddenly ordered. "I'm driving you back to your mobile home."

There was no need for him to repeat his instructions. Of course, she'd comply. Gladly. The plan suited her perfectly. She'd done her research. Once inside the van, he wouldn't be able to enter unless invited. Yeah, like that was going to happen any time soon. She threw the robe onto the settee. The humans turned their backs to give her privacy. The vampire followed every moment with his glacial eyes. Did he expect to see the medallion or was he simply enjoying the view? Hard to gauge. His expression gave no indication.

"Okay, I'm ready." She informed the other humans. "Sorry for the inconvenience." She motioned towards Susie's tiny bulge. "Good luck with the kid. You won't be seeing me again."

Christoff grabbed her right elbow and hurried her to the door and out onto the street, but not before she heard Terry call back, "I wouldn't be so sure about that."

****

"What did he mean by that?" she asked Christoff as he depressed the car door key.

"Shut up and get in."

"Nice ride." She slipped into the passenger seat of the steel blue Porsche and wiggled her bottom on the dark grey, leather upholstery. As she reached to touch the dashboard screen, he pushed her hand away.

"Keep your hands to yourself."

"Hey, the same thing goes for you, asshat." His touch had surprised her. Cold as ice, yet it stung like a burn. She rubbed the skin on her hand and stared out of the window. He drove like a real Porsche owner should.

Like she would if she could ever amass a fortune. Top speed. The scenery became a blur of colors as they sped through the back roads. Towards … wait a minute. Where was he taking her? She lifted her chin and strained to see over the tops of the houses. Expensive houses. Beyond the line of roofs, she could just make out a line of azure blue water. This wasn't the way back to the forest. Why weren't they going back to the van?

"You're going the wrong way." She informed him as the pace of her erratically beating heart quickened. What was he planning to do to her? Panic set in. If only she had something heavy to throw at him. The interior of the car was immaculate. No surprise there, considering the way he dressed. If only he'd left an empty glass bottle on the floor.

"I know the way." His attention remained focused on the road ahead. His hands firmly on the steering wheel, but somehow she knew he watched her. Watched every movement.

The car slowed and turned towards a large brick wall. Iron gates opened as if their arrival had been expected and her captor drove through the decorative entrance towards the biggest mansion she'd ever seen. Her lips parted, but words escaped her. Did Chris own this palace? Her excitement waned as they passed the house and continued up the driveway.

"Fuck no." She sat bolt upright, staring out of the window. Her hands pressed firmly on the glass. "I don't believe you did this. You had no right."

There, parked beside a lovely, average-sized house, sat her campervan. An eyesore in an otherwise beautiful setting.

"I did my research. You can't get in my home without my permission. How did you drive it here?"

"I haven't been inside your home, I had it towed."

"Who owns this place? Is it yours?" Maybe she could convince the owner to help her escape?

Christoff remained silent, ignoring her questions as he slipped from the car to open the passenger door.

She jumped from her seat, rushing to the cabin of her mobile home. Once safely in the driver's seat, she grabbed her keys from inside the hole in the vinyl upholstery and tried the ignition. Nothing. Nada. Not a peep. She tried again. Same result.

He leaned against the driver's window. She could have sworn she saw the hint of a smile on his face as he told her, "I believe you'll find the engine in the garage of the main house."

"You bastard!" she screamed as she threw open the door and jumped from the cabin, fists flying. He barely flinched as she rained blows to his chest. "You can't keep me here. My ... I'm expected somewhere."

He caught her hands as she raised them for the next assault, holding them against his chest. "Then give me the medallion and I'll arrange to have the engine replaced."

What choice did she have? Her mother needed her. Needed the money for her next treatment. She had to find a way out of this place, fast.

"Stay!" she ordered with a pointed finger before she marched up the three steps to her home and unlocked the door. "I'll be back in a minute."

But, as she entered the weather-beaten home, she turned, held up her right arm, flexed her fist and slapped her bicep in an undignified salute. "You can kiss my ass, blood sucker. I'll figure out a way to escape, and when I do, I'll stake you where the sun don't shine."

She slammed the door, turned so her back rested against the fiberglass, and let her despair, and the weight of her body drag her down. When her bottom hit the floor, she cupped her face with her hands and sobbed. "What now?"

Chapter Four

Christoff leaned against the brick exterior wall of his temporary home and waited. He checked his watch for the third time in an hour and growled. What was she doing? Surely it wouldn't take an hour to find the medallion? His position gave him a beautiful view of the beach, but he rarely took pleasure in the picturesque scene other than to gauge how long before he'd be forced back into the cottage with its block-out blinds. The tinge of pink on the horizon warned him, you're almost out of time.

Damn that gypsy. He considered pounding on her door. Demanding she obey his commands. He shook his head. As if she'd pay attention to his threats. This woman had a mind of her own. She'd do as she liked without a care for anyone but herself. While he waited impatiently outside the locked door, she was probably formulating a plan to escape. Well, let her try. She couldn't get far without her van and, even with a twelve-hour head start, he'd easily catch up. Besides, he loved a good chase, the perk of his job. Hunting down and punishing the guilty his only pleasure since his death.

With a shrug and a muttered curse, he took one last look at the closed door of the van and entered his temporary home, slamming the door behind him. The blinds were already closed, the room as dark as he had left it. Susie had argued that he might take pleasure in the view from his balcony, but the manicured gardens held no appeal. His only use for foliage was as camouflage. Neither did he have any use for the king-size bed which had remained untouched since he'd arrived in Azure Waters. He neither needed nor desired sleep and hadn't since the day the vampire took away his life and that of his young wife.

He'd given up blaming himself for her death, knowing now the will and strength of a vampire to be more formidable than that of a mortal. Ingrid's fate had been sealed from the moment the vampire arrived in their small coastal chiefdom in Denmark in 1066. The memory of his wife had begun to fade. He could barely recall her features. They'd only been married a few months when her life had been taken and he'd only known her a week before the wedding. He sprawled across the couch, his arm over his eyes as he tried to remember his young wife.

A flicker of a memory surfaced. A comely, heart shaped face with cornflower blue eyes and straw-colored hair woven into long braids. Her slender body concealed by a shapeless shift drawn at the waist by a linen apron. He imagined her soft moans of pleasure as she lay quietly beneath him and the gentleness in her speech. But the image blurred then changed into the face of the gypsy, her olive skin and dark hair in complete contrast to that of his wife. As was the color of her eyes. Eyes as dark as pitch. He shook his head, trying unsuccessfully to shake the images from his mind. As if he could. Since she stood defiantly before him in Susie's living room, almost naked in her flimsy excuse for undergarments, he'd struggled to think of anything else. Had Susie not intervened, he'd planned to search every square inch of her body. Not for the medallion, no, the trinket was the furthest thing from his mind as he reached for her. Her arousal called to him, dared him, urged him to slip his fingers inside the damp crotch of her panties and stroke her swollen clit. Even now, his fingers itched to drive inside her, his thumb longed to massage her arousal, his eyes to watch her face contort with pleasure while she came against the palm of his hand. He imagined the weight of her breasts in his hands as he squeezed the DD orbs until she begged for mercy.

Enough.

Springing to his feet, he adjusted the crotch of his jeans and cursed himself. For centuries, he'd prided himself on his self-control. He'd worked hard to establish a reputation for being unemotional, driven, a loner. Other vampires feared him, and he'd earned the name Enforcer for good reason. He took pride in his work, never deviating from his plan until evil had been punished. Until now. How was this gypsy, this witch able to break through his defenses? Had she placed a spell on him? Through clenched teeth, he growled a warning.

"You *will* give me that medallion, wench, and remove the spell you've cast over me or I will end your sorry life."

****

For the longest time, she sat with her back to the door, staring at the wall safe. The vampire had made himself clear. He wanted the medallion and would stop at nothing to get it. Her instinct told her to give him the damned thing and skedaddle, but she was no fool. If he wanted the trinket so badly and was willing to go to great lengths to get it, it must be very valuable. She'd be crazy to part with it. How could she even contemplate giving away what might be her salvation? Her heart fluttered, and a strange sensation shook her body. It took a little while to recognize the feeling. It had been so long since she'd experienced it. Hope.

If this coveted prize was worth as much as Christoff had led her to believe, it may well be her ticket to a better life. A life where she wasn't forced to use her body as the means to an end. Where she could buy a small home somewhere, maybe find a nice guy and settle down. Closing her eyes, she drew in a deep breath and let it out slowly. With enough money, she could find a cure for her mother and still have all those things. *If*, she could lose the vampire.

No use sitting around fretting. She sprang to her feet and hurried to the wall safe where she retrieved the bag of gold trinkets and poured the contents onto the kitchen table. The charm wasn't difficult to find amongst the others. It gave off a golden, almost ethereal light which she hadn't noticed before. Holding her hand over the object, she gasped as heat radiated through her palm. Her thoughts wandered back to the night she first spotted the item and how it had burned her skin. She pulled her hand back and sat on the bench seat, staring at the unusual design. *Strange*. More like a gang tattoo than a pendant motif, the angry face of a wolf glared at her from the center of the amulet. Its bared teeth threatening from inside the first circle of pattern. The geometric design surrounding the wolf appeared to be an optical illusion. Was it an M or a W? Perhaps a W for wolf? In the outside circle, the looping ribbon seemed out of place. Evangeline screwed up her nose. Art had never been her forte, but shouldn't the geometric design have been continued? Wouldn't that have been more aesthetically pleasing? With a shrug, she continued to study the curious locket. Was that a full moon behind the wolf's head?

The longer she gazed at the piece, the more her fingers itched to open it or at least trace the design with the tips of her fingers. Something about the deeply etched engraving intrigued her, tempted her. Why had the artist carved so deeply into the metal? She leaned her elbows onto the table, her face inches away from the object, but far enough to prevent a facial burn. Both sides of the locket were sealed with no sign of an opening clasp. Why commission a locket that can't be opened? She took a butter knife from the cutlery basket on the table and flipped the piece over. Nothing. No design, no name, no artist's signature. Nada. As she turned it around with the knife, the thickness of the piece caught her attention, making the double catches even more peculiar as it indicated something inside. Something that required half an inch of metal to contain it. What could it be? Diamonds? A priceless coin? The knife dropped from her hand. A rush of adrenaline shook her body as her mouth curled into a smile. By hell or high water, she'd open this thing and claim the prize.

****

Christoff punched numbers into his cell phone as he watched the taxi pull away.

"Palmer, I need a favor."

Powerless to follow, his only course of action was to enlist the help of his colleague. The gypsy hadn't packed a bag. Possibly she'd only left to purchase food, but he couldn't take that chance. She may have the medallion with her. He had to know if his suspicion was correct. After giving the private investigator the cab license plate number, he resigned himself to a long wait.

Even with his vast police resources, it might take Palmer hours to locate the woman. Hours that gave her opportunity to leave town. Something deep inside Christoff stirred. What if he never found her. What if he never saw her again? He shook his head. Why should he even care? She meant nothing to him. He tried to convince himself that his only interest was her crimes and the medallion, but the image of her voluptuous body trickled through the carefully contrived walls protecting his sanity. She couldn't leave. Not before he'd satisfied his primal urges. He'd seen the way she tempted men with her curves. Even as she postured, half-naked in the Palmer residence, her hooded eyes and heady musk had called to him and by god, he'd been tempted. The memory of her pouting lips sent a rush of blood to his cock as he imagined how she'd probably honed her craft. This one was no shrinking violet. She'd cheerfully drop to her knees for a price. He imagined her bow-shaped mouth encircling the tip of his cock, opening wider as she took more of his shaft into her throat. Her tongue licking, sucking the essence from his body as her other hand pumped his ball sack in exquisite rhythm to her mouth. He pictured his hands in her hair, fingers clenching close to the scalp, holding her, guiding her as he groaned his approval of her technique. He threw his head back, closing his eyes as the room began to spin. Close. So close.

He saw vibrant colors, felt his muscles tighten, heard … heavy metal music?

"What!" he screamed into the cell phone as he extracted his hand from down the front of his open trousers and carefully zipped his fly. His cock pulsed angrily against the fabric. Close, but no cigar.

"Hey. You're the one who asked me to call if I had any information." Terry Palmer retaliated. "Screw you, Berg. If you don't want my help, I'll –"

"I apologize, Palmer. You caught me at an inopportune moment." Terry's curse rang in his ears. Screw you. If only the call could have waited a few more minutes. He let out a long sigh, knowing the moment had been lost. "What have you discovered?"

"She didn't leave town as you suspected. I knew she'd recognize me, so I had one of our new operatives follow her. She's been in the public library doing some sort of research in the archives and on the internet. As far as I know, she's still there."

"She's very clever," Christoff reminded his partner, "how experienced is this new private investigator? I don't want her to know we're stalking her."

"Stalking? You may stalk. We shadow."

"Whatever. Will she suspect?"

"Well, he's new to private investigation. He used to be a beat cop, but wanted a career change and I was able to convince David to give him a chance."

Christoff rolled his eyes. "Your friend had better not screw up. I want this woman."

For a moment, Palmer remained silent. Christoff immediately realized the implication.

"It's not what you think."

Laughter bubbled down the receiver. "Oh, not what I think? I think it's exactly what I think. Your Freudian slip just incriminated you, Lurch."

"I neither understand nor appreciate the Lurch reference. Nor do I agree with your insinuation." He tugged at the collar of his shirt, grateful that his sign of weakness went unwitnessed.

"Argue all you like," Terry teased, "You want this woman. You want her bad."

"Just keep me informed." Christoff pressed the "call-end" button, closing his eyes as his mouth tightened into a grimace. How could he let this happen? This woman had clawed her way into his thoughts, clouded his judgement and fired his blood. Somehow, he'd make her pay for her transgressions, after he'd satisfied his needs.

****

Evangeline dropped the pile of books onto the table and sneezed. The research section of the library seemed relatively unused and rarely dusted. Some areas had fine cobwebs strung from top to bottom. Fortunately, spiders didn't bother her.

"Bless you," whispered a handsome young man sitting to her left. She smiled her thank you and quickly ducked her head down to avoid the stern glare of the elderly woman beside him. *Hag*. To her right, she noticed an older man, around forty, dressed in a wrinkled suit that smelled of moth balls. He sat close to her. Too close. As if the camphor smell was not bad enough, his body odor and the menthol of his cigarettes turned her stomach. She used her bottom to maneuver her chair further left, making a screeching noise that echoed throughout the library. The older woman shushed her. She rewarded the woman with a middle finger salute and a sarcastic smile. The younger man blushed and stared down at his computer as the side of his mouth curled into a smile. *Cute*. Turning back to her pile of reading, she wondered what it would be like to be with a cute guy. A nice guy. She'd had her fill of sleazy old men gawking at her boobs while jerking themselves off. Look but don't touch. She'd been able to keep them under control. Mostly. Occasionally, she'd have to pull out her trusty Swiss army knife and lay down the law to some overzealous customer. So far, she'd been lucky. Besides the rare boob or crotch grab she'd managed to restrain even the most 'insistent' clients. Not that she was untouched. She'd had her fair share of boyfriends. Lost her virginity at sixteen to a twenty-five-year-old drifter who seduced her in the woods behind her mother's caravan. Since then, she'd been a 'bad boy' magnet. They wanted her for her body, she wanted them for...? Why did she always fall for the tough guys? Protection? Security? No matter. When her mother's condition deteriorated, her priorities changed.

With a swipe of her hand, she took the top layer of dust off the cover of the first book. *Wolves: The meaning behind the symbol*. She flipped to the contents page, hoping to find a reference that sounded promising. No such luck. None of the ambiguous headings offered instantaneous answers. Her shoulders slumped as she realized she'd be forced to read, or at least flick through, every page of the humungous book. All three thousand, two-hundred and fifty of them. She leaned her left elbow on the table, cupped her chin in her hand and began to search.

****

"She's still in the library?" Christoff checked his watch. "It's been nine hours since she left."

"I guess she hasn't found what she's looking for." Terry answered. "Should I call off surveillance?"

"Give me half an hour." Christoff told him as he collected his car keys from the foyer table. "Tell him to not let her out of his sight until I get there."

As he rushed from the house, he paused for a moment to study the old campervan parked a few feet from the cottage. Every inch the stereotypical gypsy caravan, he couldn't help but admire her skill. If he hadn't already checked the registration and known that the van was only ten years old, he'd have believed it to be an heirloom. He'd lived in Romania for a time, back in the day. He'd also dealt with gypsies before and punished those who dabbled in the dark arts. Most made their living from the desperate, the gullible. Fortune tellers, crystal ball readers, frauds. Some sold charms and potions, others, their bodies. These things did not concern him. The clients got what they paid for. Peace of mind, confidence, pleasures of the flesh.

A shiver trickled down his spine, but he ignored it as he pressed the ignition of his car. There would be time for pleasure later. For now, he would have to focus all his attention on finding the woman and forcing her to hand over the medallion.

****

A loud grumble drew the annoyed attention of the old hag who, once again, made her presence known with a shush.

Evangeline ignored the woman, but found it harder to ignore her rumbling stomach. She'd left her home in a hurry to get to the library. The money in her pockets barely covered the cab fare. Fortunately, the male driver accepted a flash of cleavage in place of a tip. She checked the list she'd composed from her internet research. One more book from the archives and she could call it a night. She stole a quick glance at the young man working diligently beside her. His casual, neat clothes suggested a decent job, probably a nice, inexpensive car. His hair was cut short but stylish and he smelled a hell of a lot better than moth ball man, who seemed to have disappeared. Yep. One more book and she'd convince cutie-pie to buy her a burger and drive her home.

The fluorescent light in the archive section had dimmed since her last visit. Evangeline noticed the bulb flickering in sporadic shudders and hurried to find what she wanted before the light died altogether. No such luck. As the room plunged into darkness, she felt a hand clamp around her nose and mouth. Strong hands delved into the pockets of her dress, searching, tearing at the material in a desperate rush to find something. Money? She struggled against the attack, biting the fingers of the hand that covered her mouth when the offender's other hand dug inside the cup of her bra. He grunted, tugged his fingers from between her teeth and pushed her to the floor. She screamed as she crawled towards the light of the main room, hoping someone would come to her aid before he found her in the darkness. A hand grabbed her by the ankle. She kicked out, her heel connecting with bone. A shin? The blow hit her right cheek, instantly closing her eye. Momentarily dazed, she found herself being dragged back into the shadows, defenseless, confused, terrified.

"What's going on in here?"

Evangeline struggled to her feet and fumbled her way out of the room. The bright lights in the main reading room made her swollen eye weep. She covered it with her hand as she surveyed the empty room. Fear gripped her by the throat and squeezed. She'd hoped to coax the young man into buying her a meal. Now, she'd be happy with a ride home, even from the cranky old woman. Where had they all gone?

"Are you alright, Miss?" The librarian asked when Evangeline dropped her hand from her eye.

"Someone attacked me in there." The tremor in her voice surprised her. *Can't lose it, not here.*

"I didn't see anyone," the librarian told her with a frown. "Besides you."

Evangeline looked past the woman and into the dark room. Her legs began to give way as she realized. "He must be still in there."

"I'll get you a glass of water." the other woman suggested. Her expression looked anything but concerned.

"You don't believe me?" Was it her own version of the boy who cried wolf? Had she told so many lies, they were no longer convincing? She pointed to her face. "Do you think I did this to myself?"

"It's possible that, when the bulb blew, you walked into a shelf." Her expression turned from stoic to cautionary. A sneer curled the corner of her mouth. "I assure you that our insurance company has dealt with 'falls' before. If you'd like me to call the police, I'd be happy to oblige. I think they'd probably want to have a word with you."

"That won't be necessary." Evangeline threw back her shoulders and swallowed the lump in her throat. She knew exactly what the librarian was inferring. No-one would believe her story. As always, she would be suspected, ridiculed, even despised. They'd smirk as they listened to her story and snicker amongst themselves. Maybe not to her face, although it wouldn't be the first time, but they would believe she'd either brought it on herself or made up the entire story.

She grabbed her bag from the table and held it open. "Would you like to check it?"

The woman shook her head and looked away. "It's closing time, miss."

"That's okay." Evangeline told her with a shrug. "I know when I'm not welcome."

She hurried through the building, fighting back the tears of anger, tears of shame and slammed straight into a cold, solid wall of muscle.

****

"Why the rush?"

"Look, Chris. I've had a bad day. Piss off and leave me alone." She tried to skirt around him, but he wasn't finished with her.

"Bad day? What, no one succumbed to your sexuality? You must be losing your touch."

He expected an argument or, at the very least, a sarcastic rebuke. What he didn't expect was a torrent of tears. The large bag in her hand dropped to the pavement and her body collapsed down with it. She held her palms to her face, sobbing as tremors shook her body. Words eluded him. Dropping down to one knee, he placed a hand on her shoulder.

"Come. I will take you back to your trailer."

She lifted her chin, tears streaming down her face as she brushed a bothersome curl of thick black hair from her left eye and winced. "Thank you."

He grabbed her shoulders, his blood boiling as he stared at the swollen, red eyelid. "Who has done this to you?"

One huge ebony eye stared back at him, the other almost closed shut. Her mouth formed a perfect O as she gasped, "Your eyes! They're blood red."

He turned his head away. Despite centuries of practice, he was yet to master the ability to hide his rage, and more recently, his arousal. Damn her bountiful curves. Without a word, he raised her to her feet and hung the oversized bag over her shoulder.

She brushed the debris from her skirt and drew in a deep breath as she straightened her shoulders. His heart skipped a beat as he studied the rise and fall of her breasts.

"Eyes up here, big boy," she told him, her voice beginning to regain the feisty zing of confidence.

When their eyes met, he repeated his question. "Who did this to you?"

Her shoulders raised in a shrug and her mouth tightened into a straight line. "Fucked if I know. One minute I'm watching the light bulb about to blow in the archive room. The next, some low-life has one hand over my mouth and the other down my shirt."

Christoff's inner demon roared, but he managed to control the tone and volume of his voice as he asked, "Did he molest you?"

She shook her head, then winced, before holding her palm to her eye. "I fought back, even managed to plant a good kick to, what I suspect was his shin. That's when the bastard punched me."

What manner of man strikes a woman? A coward. A sorry excuse for a human man who needs to be punished. He swallowed down the anger like a bitter pill, needing to stay calm, ask more questions.

"How did you escape?"

She flipped some wayward curls behind her ears, exposing her long, smooth neck. Blood drummed in his ears making it hard to hear her answer. He asked her to repeat it.

She sighed and rolled her eyes. "As I said. The librarian came to the door and called out. He must have run out a different way because she denied seeing anyone but me."

"Surely someone in the library heard or saw something?"

"Nope. By the time I got my shit together, the library was empty."

Empty? Where was the investigator send to follow Evangeline? His temper cooled to a slow burn. He and Terry Palmer were going to have words. Strong words.

"Listen, Chris. How about that lift? I'm feeling a bit…"

He caught her by the elbow as she swayed and buckled a little at the knees. What had that monster done to her?

"Have you other injuries? Do you need a doctor?"

With a wave of her hand, she dismissed his concerns.

"I'm just hungry I guess. I haven't eaten since yesterday morning."

How could he have been so selfish? He'd kept her sequestered in her mobile home and never bothered to enquire if she had adequate provisions to sustain her life. Was there nothing left of his humanity? Was he really the monster she'd accused him of being?

"Come, we shall purchase some food on the way home." He handed her his mobile phone. "There are many fine restaurants in this area. Order whatever you wish and ask them to pack it to go. We shall pick it up on the way through."

She took the phone from his hand, an odd

expression on her face. Had she not understood his instructions? Was she unable to operate the device?

"Anything?" Her eyes sparkled with delight. "Really? I can order whatever I want? Money's no object?"

"Come," he cupped her elbow and led her up the path to where he'd parked his Porsche. "You order while I drive."

****

"Want some? I told them to hold the garlic."

She held out the half-empty pizza box as she stuffed another piece into her mouth. He shook his head, content to watch her eat. Where did she put all that food?

"Suit yourself." Although still chewing on a chunk of mozzarella covered pepperoni and jalapeno supreme, she managed to squeeze in a couple of fries and swallow it down with a slurp of chocolate milkshake.

He looked down at his previously immaculate coffee table and sighed. Strewn across the table, he counted two cheese stained pizza boxes, two milkshake containers, an empty carton of fries and a bag of corn chips.

A huge smile spread across her face as she patted her distended belly and sighed. "Thanks, Chris. That really hit the spot."

He studied her through knit brows. She actually enjoyed eating that garbage?

"I did make it clear you could order whatever you wanted, didn't I?"

Crossing her arms over her belly, she dipped her chin and looked up at him with doe eyes as she waved towards the mess.

"Behold, the evidence. Food of the gods."

He grunted his reply. "I can't imagine a god choosing to eat *this* over five-star cuisine." He sat forward in his seat. "You do realize we passed three fine restaurants on the way here. Wouldn't you have preferred to order lobster or fillet mignon?"

"I've never eaten that stuff." She took another drag on the straw of her milkshake. "Don't even know what the last thing you said is."

"Steak. Well prepared steak."

"Oh, yeah. I've heard steak is pretty good. I do enjoy a good hamburger."

She stared down at the unfinished food as though contemplating eating more. Her insatiable appetite amazed him and made him wonder about her sexual appetite. Was that also insatiable?

"I'm done." She flopped back against the settee and belched. "Ah, that's better."

The entire scene perplexed him. Yes, the curves and hooded eyes still held allure, but she'd let down her guard. Her body language relaxed and casual. Did she no longer consider him a threat?

Standing, he began to clean up the remains of the meal. "If you've finished, I'll dispose of the—"

She leapt from the couch and stilled his hands. Her touch sent a bolt of electricity through his body.

"Where I come from, what isn't eaten for dinner is served for breakfast."

He could hardly believe his ears. "Pizza for breakfast? Surely you jest?"

"I never joke about food."

She took the boxes from him and cradled them in her lap as though they were her precious babies. When her pout mutated into a forced smile, he knew she was about to ask a favor.

"Do you think I could store these in your refrigerator? Mine's been on the blink for a month now."

"A month?" Surely the perishables need

refrigeration. How could she manage? "Aren't you concerned with food poisoning from your left-over food?"

"Left overs?" Her mouth curled on one side, but her smile never reached her eyes. "I live on a diet of crackers and tins of tuna. No refrigeration necessary."

"That's no way to live." He had meant to offer counsel, but even to his own ears, his words sounded condescending. Small wonder she instantly threw up an invisible barrier between them. A divide that warned him he'd disrespected her way of life.

"Well, I have no choice." She retaliated with fire in her dark eyes. "Some of us weren't born with a silver spoon in our mouth."

He opened his mouth to speak, but reconsidered. What good would come from telling her that, he too had once lived from hand to mouth, fighting and stealing for scraps?

They remained silent for some time, an awkward standoff until she broke the stalemate.

"Hey, Chris." She lowered her chin as she spoke in gentle tones. "Thanks. Thanks for the meal and the ride."

He wanted to tell her how much he enjoyed watching her devour her meal or simply lean forward and lick the dribble of pizza sauce off her chin. He did neither. Big mistake.

"If you truly wished to thank me, you could save us both more drama and hand over the medallion."

****

"You really are a piece of work!" She rose to her feet and glared down at him. "I'm impressed. You had me fooled and that doesn't happen often. Kudos to you." She slapped her hands together in praise, but pictured them connecting with his face. Hard. "I almost believed you were a nice guy."

"You were wrong."

"No shit."

Anger bubbled up from the depths of her soul. She'd trusted him, allowed herself to believe he actually cared about her. How could she be so stupid? He'd always made his intentions clear. He wanted the medallion and the treasure inside. Any indication of more had been fabricated in her own desperate mind. It was not lust in his eyes, not for her anyway. She should have recognized the signs and guarded her heart.

"Well, it ain't gonna happen so get over it." With a defiant flick of her hair, she turned and headed for the front door. He caught her by the wrist and pulled her hard against his chest.

"Where do you think you're going?"

The musk of his body overwhelmed her senses. She wanted to push him away, scream obscenities, do something. Anything. Instead, she breathed him in and concentrated on the erratic beating of his heart.

"I thought," she whispered against his chest, "I believed vampires' hearts didn't beat."

"If that were true, then why would we need blood to sustain us?"

She pushed against his body but left her palms on his broad, solid chest. "You really are strange."

He frowned, but she could see the hint of a smile tweaking the corners of his mouth. "How so?"

"I don't know how to explain it, but somehow I believe that you'd answer any of my questions honestly."

"Why would you think otherwise?"

She dropped her hands and took a step back. "In my vast experience dealing with people, honesty is not a common characteristic."

Christoff laughed, slapping his thighs. "Vast

experience? How old are you anyway? Twenty-five, twenty-six?"

"I'm twenty-seven. How old are you?"

"I'll let you do the math," he teased. "I was born in 1036."

"You're fucking kidding me." She held her palms to her cheeks and tried to work out the centuries, but math had never been her strong point. Her formal education ended the year her mother fell ill. She left school at age 12. "This may take me a while."

He crossed his arms over his chest, but his expression showed no signs of judgement. "If it helps, I died at the age of thirty."

"Okay, I can deal with that." She thought for a minute. Would he really answer all her questions honestly? "Next question. Why do you want my amulet? Is it valuable?"

He narrowed his eyes, looking down at her from their six-inch height difference. His nose, impossibly straight compared to her slightly deviated septum. She fought the urge to cover her imperfections. How could her dark eyes, olive skin and unruly hair compare to his perfect complexion, ice-blue eyes and cropped, wheat blond hair? Even as she looked up into his face, she could feel the swelling closing her left eye. What a sight she must be. His answer shook her back to reality.

"It is not your amulet. You stole it from the pawn shop owner along with numerous other items. But in fairness, he got more satisfaction from the deal than you."

Heat rushed to her face. "You … you saw?"

He nodded his answer and she glimpsed a twinkle in his eye that scorched her cheeks.

She turned her face away from his gaze. "Why is it so valuable?"

"Monetarily, it holds no value."

She spun around. "Then why are you holding me prisoner here?"

"Because the amulet is dangerous. Surely with your unusual powers, you've sensed that."

Evangeline rubbed her palm. Of course, she'd sensed the energy in the locket. She'd spent the evening staring at the unusual design and the following day researching it. But could she trust this man, this vampire?

"Cut the crap, Chris. There's more to this locket than you're telling me." She dug her fingers into her hips and took a deep breath. "I'm prepared to sell you the locket, for a price."

His answer surprised her.

"Name it."

Well, that was easier than I thought. He must be desperate. "No, you start the ball rolling. Make me an offer and we'll go from there."

"Ten thousand dollars."

"Ten thousand?" She heard the catch in her voice and silently berated herself. That was the starting offer? How high would he go?

"Sorry, sweet cheeks." She raised her hand, palm up and motioned higher. "Keep going."

His expression remained stoic. "Thirty thousand dollars."

Her heart beat double-time as she tried to raise the bid. "Fifty thousand. And, a steak dinner."

He tilted his head to one side and frowned. "You're still hungry?"

She balled her hand into a fist and tapped it to his forehead. "Tomorrow you bring me fifty thousand cash and take me to one of those fine places you talked about. Then, I'll give you the amulet."

He held out his hand, which she accepted. When he refused to let go, she squared her shoulders and looked up at him with her good eye.

"Was there something else?"

"I agree to those terms, but only if you agree to my conditions."

Her breath hitched. What did he want from her? Blood?

"What conditions?"

He pulled her in closer, his cheek against hers as he whispered into her ear. "I want the same deal as the pawn broker."

Evangeline gasped as a wave of molten heat travelled down her navel and pooled between her legs. Her breasts felt impossibly heavy. Arousal soaked her panties.

"You want me to—"

"Yes, min dyrebare. You will strip for me, but make no mistake, I am nothing like that loathsome degenerate. Don't expect me to be satisfied by a glimpse of bosom. I want to see all of you. Every last inch of your flesh. Those are my conditions."

Evangeline's mind raced. She could do so much with that money. Good doctors for her mother. A deposit on a real home. She sideways glanced at Christoff. It would make a nice change to strip for a real man. A hot, toned, hunk of a man. Why then, did the prospect make her feel so dirty? What else did he expect for his money? She pushed her indignation to the back of her mind. *Mum needs me*. The pain in her heart was harder to ignore. She'd have given him her body, her heart, her soul. If only he'd treated her with some respect. Lifting her chin, she met his shameless stare and made a decision. He'd get his striptease, maybe even a lap dance if she felt inclined, but first, she'd find out what was inside that locket.

She forced a smile, thrusting out her chest as she

raised herself onto her toes to position her lips close to his.

"Shall we seal our pact with a kiss?"

He edged closer, his breath on her mouth, his lips tantalizingly close, his eyes as wide as saucers. Then, he backed away.

"Tomorrow."

She tried to decipher his expression. Was he angry? She opened her mouth to ask him and was interrupted.

"It's nearly dawn, and I think it best you return to your own accommodation. Tomorrow I will come for you at 7:00 PM. Be ready." He turned and headed towards his bedroom, stopping at the door to add a final warning. "Do not believe I can be swayed by your feminine wiles. You will honor our pact or there will be consequences."

Chapter Five

"Do you know what time it is?"

"Of course." Christoff answered. "I do own a watch."

"I forgot who I was talking to, and please don't respond to that, it was rhetorical."

Christoff sighed. Humans. If he lived another thousand years, he'd never understand them.

"Listen, Palmer. I want the name and address of the man you paid to follow Evangeline. He needs to be taught a lesson."

"Wait just a minute." Terry cleared his throat. "What lesson? What are you talking about?"

"I asked you to have her followed, not beaten. Your lackey sexually assaulted her and blackened her eye. I will not tolerate such behavior." He could feel the tension knotting his shoulders and he struggled to control the volume of his speech.

"No way." Terry argued. "My man is a pussy cat with women. When he phoned in his surveillance report he couldn't stop commenting on how nice she seemed. He said he left the moment she walked into a different room of the library."

"If not him, who attacked her?"

"Give me a minute to leave the room," Terry asked, "I don't want to wake Susie."

Within minutes, the volume of his voice changed.

"Okay, I've just checked my computer, and in his report, Adam mentioned two other people sitting at the same table with him and your gypsy. Another man and an older woman. One of those could have been the unsub."

"I will give your colleague the benefit of the doubt, for now." *But I'll be keeping an eye on him.*

"Gee, thanks." The sarcasm in Terry's voice was clear, even to Christoff. "Now, fuck off back to your coffin and stop calling me at three in the morning."

The line went dead. Christoff shrugged and strolled to the refrigerator for a snack.

The left-over slices of pizza glared at him from the almost empty shelves inside the refrigerator as he reached for his morning bag of blood. He raised an eyebrow, pondering Evangeline's choice of food. Given cart-blanche, she chose fast food? He shook his head. It didn't make sense. He'd followed her for weeks. Watched her steal and blackmail, extort, and demand exorbitant amounts of money from unsuspecting customers. Why then didn't her lifestyle reflect this? She'd told him her refrigerator was out of order. Surely that would be a priority? Even her clothes bore the tags of bargain basement stores. He'd caught a glimpse of the tag at the base of her neck, while whispering his terms into her ear. He scratched his chin and wondered if she even had clothes suitable for the restaurant he'd planned to take her to this evening. Should he ask? The image of her proud face materialized in his mind. He shook the idea from his thoughts and decided on a better course of action.

****

What's that noise? Evangeline stretched her arms above her head and checked the time on her phone. 9:00 AM. Sleeping had proven difficult after the events of the previous day and especially the night. Even her dreams had been disturbingly X-rated. Her nipples strained against the cotton tank top. Her satin boxers clung uncomfortably against her skin, damp from the memory of her dream lover's hands stroking her, teasing her, tasting her.

Bang, bang, bang.

"All right, I'm coming!" She called to the intruder at her door. A smile spread across her face. If the caller had waited a few minutes longer...

"Who is it?" The chain provided enough room to peek through the crack. She hoped it would give her enough time to slam and lock the door if her attacker had found her.

"I have a delivery for Ms. Evangeline Russo."

"I didn't order anything." What was this young guy playing at? Was it a trap?

"The invoice says it's from a Mr. Christoff Berg. I need a signature."

Chris? *What would he have sent me?* Interesting. She closed the door, unlatched the chain, and flung the door open, posing with one hand on the handle, the other on her hip. Judging by the delivery man's face, he appreciated the view and the size of his package impressed her as well. Was there a body in that box?

"Sign here please." The young man stammered as he held out the electronic device and stylus.

As she handed back the apparatus, she grabbed the package and after struggling to squeeze it into the door frame, shut the door behind her. Absently, she called her thanks through the door as she began to tear into the box. A gift, for me? When was the last time she'd received anything by courier? Come to think of it, not once. She'd never stayed in a location long enough to have an actual postal address and for good reason. For the longest time, she stared at the pale pink tissue paper wrapping and the magenta ribbons binding the parcel. Whatever it was, it looked too pretty to open. Too pretty for a woman who made a living from seducing men into doing her bidding. No. Red suited her better. Scarlet like the label she'd been given.

She sat cross-legged on the linoleum floor and

gently untied the bows, gasping when the prize was revealed. A dress? Not *just* a dress, a beautiful, mint green dress made from the softest fabric she'd ever touched. Her fingers skimmed the material. As smooth as butter. Carefully, she lifted it from the box and held it up to the full-length mirror near her bed. The full skirt sat at a modest length, just below her knees, but nothing else about the dress suggested modesty. Beside the band of fabric behind the neck, it was otherwise backless, and the plunging neckline left little to the imagination, opening to the waist. She returned to the empty box, searching for a note and found an envelope addressed to her. Inside, along with a note, she discovered a satin thong in the same color as the dress. Her eyebrows knit as she examined the skimpy underwear. Hardly more than a scrap of lace and a few ribbons of satin. Her hand shook as she read the note aloud.

"I have taken the liberty to choose an appropriate ensemble for you in preparation for our dinner and my après dinner entertainment."

Après dinner? Her hand shot to her mouth as she remembered the whispered addendum.

"Don't expect me to be satisfied by a glimpse of cleavage. I want to see all of you. Every last inch of your flesh."

She held up the panties between finger and thumb and swallowed the lump caught in her throat. He'd left nothing to chance. The plunging neckline of the dress insured she'd be braless and, for the amount of flesh this thong would cover, she may as well be altogether naked. Blood pumped a steady, rhythmic beat in her ears, but her heart left enough to send to every erogenous zone in her body. This man knew exactly what he wanted and for now, he wanted her. Would that change once he had his precious locket? Would he use her body and discard her like trash? She looked from the dress back to her reflection in the mirror. Her last boyfriend had told her she had a body for sin. Despite this, he'd stolen her savings and left. With a shake of her head, she placed the dress carefully on the bed and moved her meager clothes in the wardrobe to reveal the wall safe. As she dug out the bag containing the locket, she made up her mind. He could have her body. Hell, if his body was any indication of his lovemaking, she might even enjoy it, but if he wanted the contents of that locket, he'd better be willing to pay.

****

Evangeline tossed the clumsy oven mitts aside and glared at the locket. She flipped it over with a pocket knife and studied it through the magnifying glass she'd found in a thrift store. No visible opening on either end. Who the hell designed this idiotic thing? The wall clock warned her that time was running out. Chris wanted his pound of flesh at precisely 7:00 PM. She had less than an hour to shower and dress for their rendezvous. With a sigh, she reached out with her bare left hand, and picked up the locket, wincing as the metal seared her skin.

Digging the point of the knife into the right side of the clasp, she wriggled and prodded the lock, hoping to break it open. Maybe Chris won't notice the marks on the metal? He'd only seen the medallion through the window of the caravan. She'd tell him she'd found it that way. What choice did he have but to believe her?

With one final shove, the knife slipped past the join and into the soft flesh of her palm. Blood pooled into the intricate engravings on the face of the locket. For one startling moment, the wolf's eyes flamed to life and then, the entire motif flooded scarlet as Evangeline's blood filled every crevice. Then, just as quickly, the blood disappeared, as if swallowed by the carnivorous wolf.

"Fuck. That's weird."

The locket dropped to the table and sprang open, revealing a tiny metal scroll. She ran to the tiny bathroom, tore a few sheets of toilet paper from the roll and balled it in her left hand as she warily removed the cylinder with her right hand. No sooner had she removed it, when the locket snapped shut, leaving no sign of ever having opened. Tempting as it was to unroll the tiny treasure, she realised that risk of discovery was too real. If she kept Chris waiting, he'd surely snoop around, possibly spot the scroll. No. Better to hide it away in the safe until later. In the morning, she'd have plenty of privacy and the time to research its value. Tonight, held more important issues, like … how to seduce a vampire and survive.

****

"All right, already. Don't get your knickers in a twist."

Christoff screwed up his face at the strange comment. What did she mean by that reference? He'd merely knocked repeatedly on her door. After all, she should have expected him. He checked his wrist watch. 7:00 PM precisely. He raised his hand to knock again, but it opened before his knuckles reached the door.

"I hope these sandals look okay with the dress," she told him as she posed in the doorway. "Normally, I prefer sneakers, and these are my only heels."

He took a moment to answer, afraid his voice would betray him.

"No one will be looking at your feet."

Raising his right arm, he offered her his hand and helped her down the metal steps. Her small, olive skinned hand appeared delicate in his large, pale one. Delicate, except for the small rectangular dressing on her palm and the pink, blistered skin surrounding it.

"You're hurt?"

She pulled her hand away, hiding it behind her back as if the sight of it lessened her appeal. A smile threatened to spread his lips. If anything, the action straightened her shoulders, forcing her chest forward and drawing even more attention to her breasts.

"Hey, eyes up here," she reminded him with a sweep of her hand before answering his question. "I had an accident with a knife this afternoon. Nothing major."

He regarded her facial expression with wonder. Why had she denied the burn? He'd seen enough scorched flesh in his time, usually his own, and recognized the significance. Shame closed his eyes. He'd instructed her to bring the medallion and thereby caused her injury. The drawstring purse at her wrist bore the telltale weight of a locket. He'd seen the blasted thing glowing with preternatural heat and her reaction to it. How could he have been so insensitive to her human fragility? She must have burned her hand as she placed it in her bag, as per his instructions. Drawing in a deep breath, he opened his eyes and drank her in. Her huge doe eyes, staring at him in wonder. Her full, bow-shaped lips slick with pink gloss and just a hint of perspiration. The slight deviation in her septum, an imperfection that made her even more perfect in his eyes. Round, rosy cheeks, accentuated by a strong jaw and chin. He tilted his head to the right. Why had he never noticed the widow's peak of her forehead and the way it forced her features into the shape of a heart? Of course. Her thick, unruly hair had been carefully pinned in an up style with the exception of a few wayward strands that had escaped to fall around her face.

"You look lovely, min dyrebare." He again offered his arm, elbow out. "Come, our table awaits."

She accepted his arm and allowed him to lead her

towards his car, but he sensed reluctance, a slowing of her step, until she finally stopped at the car and confessed.

"Look, Chris. I appreciate the dinner invitation, but couldn't we just order out?"

"No. We have reservations." He held firm to her elbow and tried to edge her closer to the car. She dug in her heels.

"It's just... I've never..." Genuine fear widened her already huge eyes. Fear that he could put to rest.

"If it puts your mind at ease. I have never eaten in a restaurant either."

Her mouth formed the shape of an O and she blinked a few times. "You haven't been in a restaurant? But I thought—"

"Oh, I've been in restaurants," he corrected, "I just don't eat."

Her eyebrows drew into a frown. "Stop messing with my head."

He leaned back against the side of his Porsche and folded his arms. "I can, and sometimes do eat human food, but it is not necessary for my survival. I do not eat at restaurants because I do not enjoy eating alone. Tonight will be a night of many firsts ... for both of us."

"Many?" Her face visibly paled and he heard the sharp intake of her breath as he leaned in close to her face.

"Many."

****

"Oh, shit, shit, shit." Evangeline lowered her chin and avoided eye contact with the couple about to pass their table.

Christoff leaned forward and, with the tip of his finger, raised her chin. "Back straight. Eyes forward. They will not recognize you."

She reluctantly did as he instructed, but held her breath. Would they cause a scene? Maybe have her thrown out before she'd even ordered?

As they passed, the male nodded to Christoff and the female smiled, but they followed their waiter to their table without a word. What just happened?

"Did you use some type of mind control?"

"Why would you think that?"

"I expected... I don't know what I expected." She shrugged her shoulders and scratched at the base of her neck.

"Stop that."

She dropped her hands into her lap, silently cursing herself for obeying him. Why should she care what he thinks? This was a business transaction, nothing more. Remember that, she instructed the butterflies that had taken flight in her stomach from the moment they'd arrived at the fancy schmancy restaurant. So many knives and forks, not to mention the glasses. How many glasses did one person need? The waiter handed her a menu and the butterflies dropped ... stone cold dead. Cold sweat began to bead on her upper lip and her legs turned to jelly.

He looked up from his menu, opened his mouth to speak, then paused. The coldness in his blue eyes melted away and something in her heart thawed along with it when he gently took the menu from her hand.

"Would you mind if I ordered for you? I'd like to surprise you."

She let out the breath she'd been holding and nodded. "So much to choose from. I couldn't make up my mind."

He smiled and her heart back-flipped. Why hadn't she noticed how handsome he was? Maybe because he hadn't flashed those pearly whites before? Or was it the gentleness in his features when he wasn't trying to look intimidating? He held her gaze, even as he motioned for the waiter. By the time the first course arrived, she'd fallen hopelessly in lust.

****

Despite himself, Christoff couldn't help but admire the woman. She'd adapted to the new situation with class. Mirroring his actions. Choosing the right cutlery and crystal. No wonder she'd excelled in her profession. Her people skills were excellent. If he hadn't seen her curled up on his couch, stuffing her face with pizza, he'd believe her to be every bit the lady she portrayed.

Resting his elbow on the table, he leaned his chin between his thumb and forefinger to ponder. Why choose a life of crime when she could easily use her 'talents' to snag a rich husband? She caught him staring and bit her bottom lip. Coyness? Color rushed to her cheeks and a blush spread down her neck to her breasts. *This is new.*

"Do I have something on my face?" She nervously swiped at her mouth with a napkin while avoiding eye contact.

Strange thing to say. "No. Why do you ask?"

She dropped the napkin back in her lap and frowned. "The way you were staring at me, I thought I must have grown another head."

"I don't understand humans," he shook his head while remembering, "Susie hyperventilated when I studied her face. Why are you women so nervous?"

An invisible barrier went up between them. She squared her shoulders and held her chin high, as if he'd somehow insulted her.

"I only met her once, but she is beautiful."

"Who?"

"Susie." Her eyes rolled, and she sighed. "You

said you were staring at her."

"Oh, yes. She has the strangest eye color. I have since learned that my gaze is unsettling."

She looked up at him from under a heavy fringe of dark lashes and smiled. "Really? I hadn't noticed."

He tried to fake a frown, but he could feel the corners of his mouth curl. "I am learning to understand sarcasm. You are making fun of me."

She held out her hand, thumb and forefinger slightly apart. "Just a little bit."

He leaned forward and took her hand in his.

"You are a paradox, a great mystery to me. What drove you to a life of deceit when you could be whatever you choose? Why have you not chosen a husband?"

Ebony eyes stared at him. Her face contorted into an expression he could not comprehend. Anger? Surprise? Pain? She snatched her hand away and put it in her lap.

"How is what I do any worse than a head-shrinker? They come to me with a problem and I give them peace of mind."

He leaned forward. "And what of the husbands? What do you give them?"

Her nostrils flared. "Let me tell you something, buster. They get what they deserve. A reminder to keep it in their pants or pay the piper. I'm doing the wives a favor."

"How? By having coitus with their husbands?"

He caught her hand inches from his face and held it as she shook. "Coitus? Fancy words don't make it any less of an insult. Don't play the gentleman now, Chris. It doesn't suit you."

What had he said to upset her? Had he not stated the obvious?

"What would you have me say?"

"You swear you always tell the truth. Why did you bring me here? Was it to shame me? Well, I've got news for you, asshole. I may be a lot of things but I'm not a slut. I scam the husbands, but I don't fuck them. My body is not for sale."

Her words hit him as hard as a slap. He'd made a mistake. A mistake that caused her emotional pain. Had he lived alone too long, or had he always lacked empathy? Despite her angry expression, tears brimmed her lower lashes and she rose to leave.

"Wait." He snagged her hand. "Please, wait."

She hesitated, glanced around at the sea of faces watching her, and slunk back into her seat.

"What now? Are you going to demand that striptease here in the restaurant?"

"If you did that, I would be forced to kill every other man here." She'd asked for the truth, but would she understand? She belonged to him now. "Now, shall we order dessert?"

Her left eyebrow raised, and she leaned forward on her elbow. "You're not upset?"

"Why should I be upset?"

"I've just told you that we won't be getting groiny later. Aren't you going to throw a fit or something?"

Closing the dessert menu, he shooed away the approaching waiter with a flick of his wrist. "I suggest we renegotiate our agreement."

She crossed her arms in front of her chest and he growled his disapproval until she dropped them by her sides.

"You promised me fifty thousand."

"And you shall have it."

"I only promised to take off my clothes, nothing more."

He motioned to her with a wiggle of his finger

and she leaned closer, inches from his face.

"When the time comes for us to make love, I will take your lead."

"I don't understand." She eased back in her seat, her eyes as wide as saucers. "What do you mean, 'take my lead'?"

"I will not make any advances on you unless you instruct me to do so. When we return to the cottage, you will allow me to enjoy you with my eyes and my mind, but if you want my mouth to pleasure you, and my hands to fondle your body, you must ask. Those are my terms."

A bead of sweat trickled down her forehead, tracing the shape of her jaw before dripping down between her breasts. Her sharp intake of breath aroused him, almost as much as the peaks forming at the front of her dress. He licked his lips in anticipation.

"What if I don't ask?" she gasped. "Promise me you won't hurt me, that you won't punish me."

Turning his head to the side, he motioned for the waiter. "You might enjoy my punishment." He turned slightly to wink. "And you *will* ask."

****

The face in the restroom mirror looked terrified. She blotted the sweat from her forehead and powdered her nose before applying a fresh coat of lip gloss and a spritz of perfume. No point in putting this off. She took a deep breath, opened the door, and felt the pressure of hands on her back moments before she fell forward. As she lay on the ground, stunned and confused, a woman's scream pierced the silence. Fire!

Staff charged through the swinging doors that divided the restaurant from the kitchen. Instinctively, she curled into a ball to protect her face and stomach from the stampede of feet fleeing close to her head. Above the noise, she heard him call to her, but she dared not lift her head. Something brushed her arm, then tugged at her wrist. A hand grabbed for her. Christoff?

The purse at her wrist suddenly jerked. She held tight to the cord, the skin on the inside of her fingers burning as the assailant tugged the purse from her hands. Acrid smoke began to fill the room, blinding her as she struggled to her knees and began to crawl towards the exit. She tried to call out, but smoke filled her lungs, choking away her breath. What was that? She turned in the direction of the strange sound. A child, barely older that three or four hid under a tablecloth. Flames licked at the edges of the material. With a flick of her wrist, she sent the table flying backward and crawled to the little girl.

"It's okay, honey. I'm going to get you out of here."

"Mummy." The girl cried, her cheeks already smudged with ash.

Evangeline squinted. The patrons had become little more than silhouettes in the darkened restaurant. Everything at the front of the building had been plunged into darkness. Where was the exit? The fire spread tendrils up the walls and crept across the ceiling. Soon the roof would collapse on top of them. *Do something.* She looked behind her for another way out. *Damn.* A wall of flame blocked her way. She reached out, her hand brushed a table. Something sloshed and the clink of crystal gave her an idea. She felt around until she touched the glass jug, lifted it to her mouth to be sure, then poured the water over the child's head.

"I'm sorry kid," she told the weeping girl, "but Aunty Evangeline needs to keep you nice and damp. It's going to get pretty hot. Close your eyes and hold tight." She squeezed the child close to her chest and braced herself for the heat as she prepared to run through the flames.

Strong hands grabbed her by the shoulders. "You'll never make it."

He scooped her up, child and all, and she snuggled against his chest keeping the little girl completely covered by their bodies as, in a blur of speed, he carried them outside to the street. As he lowered her to the ground, she held tight to him, sandwiching the child between them. Afraid to let go of either. Unsteady on her feet.

"Violet!"

The child raised her head and thrust out her arms. "Mummy."

Between sobs, the mother thanked them. "I was pushed out of the building when the fire started. I tried to get back in, but the firemen wouldn't let me." She kissed her child's forehead. "Thank you. Thank you both. She's all I've got. I don't know how I could have lived if anything had happened to her."

Christoff addressed the woman, but kept his gaze fixed on Evangeline. "I completely understand."

His statement surprised her, confused her. Surely, he didn't mean *her*? So far, his attention appeared to be sexually motivated. Dare she hope for more? He leaned his chin on the top of her head, his arms crushing her to his chest and she melted into his embrace.

"Are either of you hurt?"

She raised her head. The woman and child had gone. A fireman stood in their place.

She shook her head. "I'm a little battered and bruised, but otherwise okay. Christoff?"

"I am uninjured." His eyebrows knit as he turned his attention back to her, grabbing her hands to examine them. "Your fingers are bleeding and your wrist is swollen. Perhaps you should seek medical attention."

"Oh, that wasn't from the fire." She stared down at the ring of bruising at her wrist and reality set in. "Christoff! My bag! Someone stole my bag."

"You'd better report that to the police," the fireman said as he turned to leave. "Unfortunately, criminals take advantage of the chaos."

Once they were alone, she told Christoff, "This happened before all hell broke loose. I was pushed to the ground. Whoever did it, ripped the bag from my wrist." She held her chest.

"Can't. Breathe."

He scooped her up and rushed her to his car, placing her in the passenger seat.

"Calm yourself. Money can be replaced."

She closed her eyes, reminding herself to breathe. Fifty thousand dollars down the drain. So close to getting everything she'd ever wanted in life and some bastard had stolen her golden ticket. How would Christoff react to the news?

"Evangeline?"

She opened her eyes and braced herself for his reaction as she reminded him, "It was your idea to bring the medallion with me."

His hands shot out and held her by the shoulders. "The medallion was in your purse?"

"Where else did you expect me to carry it?" She cupped her breasts for effect. "This neckline plunges down to my waist, and the panties you made me wear are barely more than a triangle with strings attached."

He released her shoulders and stared into the night. "You are right. I allowed my attraction to you to get in the way of my obligations. I and I alone am to blame for this." He turned his head, his eyes cold and emotionless as he broke her heart. "I'll drive you back to your mobile home and see to it that all preparations are made to get you back on the road. I will locate the medallion myself. Our business is finished."

****

The journey home finished too soon. He wished that he could extend the trip, maybe even turn the car around and leave town, taking her with him. How could he have been so foolish? The medallion had been close enough to touch... Now, he'd let both the locket and the woman slip through his fingers.

"I'll make the necessary calls tonight and have your engine replaced in the morning." He opened the passenger door and offered his hand. She declined, stepping from the vehicle unassisted.

"So, that's the end of it?" she asked. Her cheeks flushed with color as she breathed through her nose. "I don't have what you want anymore, so I'm expendable?"

Didn't she understand? He was releasing her from her promise, she should be happy. "I thought you'd be anxious to leave."

"You promised me fifty thousand dollars. It's not my fault the medallion was stolen. I lived up to my part of the bargain."

Ah. The money. Somehow, during the course of the evening, he'd allowed himself the luxury of believing they'd connected on some level. Fool. What he'd mistaken as affection in her eyes was greed. A gold digger working out how much money she could steal from him. She was a thief, he, a monster. They probably deserved each other.

"Well, do you agree?"

"What? Did you say something?"

"Concentrate." She balled up her fist and tapped on his forehead with her knuckles.

He didn't like it.

"I offered to give you something else for the

money. Something I think might be even more valuable."

His body betrayed him, warming to the notion she may be offering herself to him. She'd proven herself to be shameless and, damn it, he still wanted her. Wanted her enough to pay the fifty thousand if that was her price. He closed the distance between them.

"Fifty thousand dollars is a large amount of money. Are you worth it?"

"Will you get your mind out of the gutter." She held him back with her outstretched arms. "I'm not offering to sell my body."

"More's the pity." He turned away, ashamed that he'd admitted his desire, given her the upper hand.

"I opened the medallion." She blurted out.

He spun around to face her. "You what? When?"

"This morning." She dropped her chin, her eyes darting from her feet to the ground. "I thought ... it looked like there might be something inside. I wanted to—"

"You wanted to rob me."

"No, I—"

"Liar." Was there no end to her deceit? "You made a deal, the money for the locket. That included anything inside it."

Color flushed her cheeks and tears brimmed her bottom lashes. "You don't understand."

"No, I understand all too well." Fake tears would not sway him from his decision. "The original terms of the agreement remain. I will have whatever it is you took from the locket." He reached for her, snagging her wrist. "I am a man of patience, but you have pushed me to my limit." Her mouth gaped open, her eyes widening as he dragged her towards the cottage. "No more games."

"Where are you taking me?" she whimpered as they stormed past the living room towards his bedroom.

"You made me a promise that you wouldn't force me to do anything."

He ignored the rapid beating of her pulse. However, the heady perfume of her arousal proved harder to overlook. This pleased him. Despite her protests, she wanted this.

"I wish to keep tonight's entertainment private." Slamming the bedroom door behind them, he sat on the edge of his bed. "The other rooms are fitted with security cameras. You promised me seductive dance, not my employers. I may be a vampire, however, I'm still a gentleman."

"Pfft." She leaned back against the door and crossed her arms. "You are no gentleman."

"And you are no lady." He mirrored her body language, crossing his arms across his chest and frowning. "Begin."

****

"I need to use the bathroom." Why did his hungry expression send her blood pumping to all her erogenous zones? *Can't breathe.*

He pointed to an ensuite and she wasted no time rushing in, closing the door behind her. Leaning over the sink, she turned on the cold water and splashed her face and neck until some of the heat dissipated. When she looked up, the mirror reflected what she already suspected. Her eyes were as wide as saucers. Her face, neck and breasts a deeper shade of tan. With a tissue she took from the box on the vanity, she patted beneath her breasts and under her arms. Why was she so nervous? She'd stripped for men many times before. Why was tonight so different? *Because, this one will not be satisfied with a glimpse of lace and a suggestive dance,* her reflection reminded her. This man would make sure he'd get his money's worth. His pound of flesh. As much as it pained her to admit it, she wanted to give it to him, and more. Much more.

"I'm waiting."

She swallowed down the anxiety, threw her shoulders back and opened the door. The mood of the room had changed, softened. Fragrant candles replaced the glare from the bright overhead lights. Soft music played from the iPod speaker on a bedside cabinet with an open bottle of sparkling white wine beside it. As she approached, he offered her a glass which she accepted without complaint, downing the entire contents in one gulp after noticing that the bedlinen had been turned back. She held out the glass for a refill and drank that as fast as the first.

"Begin." He leaned back on the bed, his shirt gaping just enough for her to notice the definition of his abs.

She felt the sting as her top teeth bit into her bottom lip. Why did he have to look so hot?

His frown warned her that he wouldn't ask again. She began to sway to the music, hoping to find confidence in the beat of the slow ballad. It began to work. She closed her eyes, gyrating her hips in time to the music, losing herself in the moment as her hands molded the contours of her body.

"Open your eyes."

She did as instructed, meeting his gaze with the same intensity. In that moment, she felt his compulsion, his control, his hands.

"How are you doing that?" she gasped as the pressure of invisible fingers traced her spine.

"Relax."

Her body obeyed his words immediately. Warmth spread over her skin beneath the touch of his mind control. Try as she might to hate that he'd tricked her, she couldn't help but enjoy the sensation of ghostly hands fondling her flesh. Damn him.

"You said you wouldn't touch me."

"With my hands."

Memories of their earlier conversation flooded back. He'd promised to enjoy her with his eyes and mind. How was she to know what he could do with them? "This isn't fair. You're controlling me."

"Tit for tat, my dear. How does it feel to have someone manipulate you like a marionette? Now, take down your hair."

Her hands reached up to slide the clip holding her hair in the up-style, spilling dark curls down below her shoulders.

"Good," he groaned, as she leaned down and swung her hair in a circular pattern, flipping it back in a jerk as her body kept time with the music.

Bending at the knees, she traced the outline of her right leg with her hands, from the top of her thigh, over her calf and down to her ankle. When she reached her sandal, she slipped it off and did the same on the left leg. As she straightened, her hands reached behind her neck and loosened the bow holding the dress in place. His breath hitched, or was it hers, as she brought the straps forward, lowering the dress until her breasts were half exposed.

He squirmed on the edge of the bed, leaning forward as she turned her back and let the dress fall to her waist.

"If you tease me," he warned as her nipples felt the tug of incorporeal fingers, "you will force me to inflict unimaginable pleasure."

"*Unimaginable* pleasure?" she repeated absently, as unseen hands lifted the weight of her breasts and squeezed. Dare she test him? After all, she did have a vivid imagination. Instead, she grasped the waistband of her dress, bent at the middle gifting him full view of her ample behind as she tugged the dress down over the lace thong, to her ankles and stepped out. Turning slowly, her hands covering her breasts, she kicked the dress at his head, using her telekinetic powers to ensure it wrapped around his face.

Without a word, he removed the dress from his face, shaking his head as a grin spread across his face.

"I did warn you."

****

So that's how she wants to play? A wicked thought sprung to mind, and his cock approved with a shudder. *I'm going to enjoy this.*

Her eyes widened, and her mouth gaped open as he sent a wave of heat down her soft belly to the pleasure nub between her legs. He'd seen her tease the pawn shop owner by pretending she was about to pleasure herself. This time, she'd perform the act. He'd make sure of it. Applying light pressure with his mind, he convinced her to remove her hands from her breasts and drop the left by her side. He had other plans for the right hand. She stared down in shock as her own hand slid inside the front of the flimsy excuse for panties and began to stroke the swollen clit, using the slickness of her own arousal to pleasure herself. As her legs began to wobble, he caught her and lowered her onto the bed while she moaned through each blissful wave.

Had he not been a man of his word, he would have torn the last scrap of fabric from her body and buried his face between her legs, but he'd given her his promise. No touching unless she asked. His plan had backfired. While she had been sated, he had Vesuvius in his trousers and it was threatening to blow.

Throwing her head back, she smiled and let out a

long sigh of satisfaction that almost caused him to spontaneously combust. Worse still, she added fuel to the fire by telling him, "That was nice, but when does the unimaginable pleasure start?"

Was it the two glasses of wine loosening her inhibitions or was she warming to the idea of making love with him? Either way, he had no complaints. She hadn't had enough alcohol to make her intoxicated, so he would not be taking advantage, and if the money was driving her desire, so be it. He would have her tonight. He matched her teasing with a taunt of his own.

"I'm the one paying fifty thousand dollars. What do I get out of this?"

She sat up and, as he held his breath, slipped out of the scant panties and scooted to the edge of the bed. When her hand squeezed his thigh, before travelling higher, he groaned his approval.

"When I dreamt of the moment you gave yourself to me, I fantasized about what I would like to do to you and have done to me."

"You fantasize about me?" She lowered herself to her knees on the floor and positioned herself between his legs, spreading his knees with her hands before massaging her way towards his crotch. "What did I do to *you*, in this daydream?"

She reached for the wine and drank from the bottle, passing it to her left hand as she continued to stroke the inside of his leg with her right.

"I think you're already reading my mind." He sighed as her fingers unbuttoned his fly and tugged the zipper down. When her hand slipped inside his satin boxers and her fingers wrapped around his shaft and tightened, he groaned his instructions. "In my fantasy, you—"

She gazed up at him, smiled, then leaned down.

As her lips touched the head of his cock, she opened her mouth. Bubbles of wine enveloped him, tantalized him, as she hummed over the sensitized tip. His breath hitched, and he closed his eyes when she cupped his balls and squeezed. Her technique flawless. The pressure perfect, even as her fingernails dug a little into his responsive sack.

"Don't stop." He opened his eyes and reached for her, threading his fingers through her hair, holding her for fear she might change her mind, but concerned his self-control may falter. He'd dreamt of this moment, the pleasure, the release. But in his fantasies, he always came inside her body, sharing the moment, giving as much as taking.

"Wait!"

When he tugged at her hair, easing her head back, her eyes widened in surprise.

"But I thought you wanted—"

"I want *you*, min dyrebare."

She sat back on her haunches, her hands on her perfectly rounded hips, her plump red lips pursed. Her disappointed expression almost brought him undone, and, when her pupils dilated as he stood and began to unbutton his shirt, he had his answer. She wanted him, too.

"Fuck this." With one almighty tug, he tore off the shirt, sending buttons flying.

He leaned down to assist her up, and, as she rose, she reached out to touch him. Her palms traced his chest and over his obliques. His abdominal muscles tightened as her fingers gripped the waistband of his trousers together with his boxers, and tugged both down his knees. Before she went any further, he gripped her shoulders.

"Allow me." He stepped out of his remaining clothes and kicked them across the room. Had her lips brushed his cock again, he would have exploded. Somehow, he suspected she already knew that. He had to take back control. Prolong the experience.

"I believe we've reached a stalemate."

"A what?" she tilted her head to one side and gazed up at him from under a fringe of long, dark lashes. Damn, she's good at her job. He tried to ignore the coquettish fluttering of her eyelashes, and the plumpness of her full, red lips, but lowering his gaze made his situation worse. Every breath she took, drew his attention to her breasts. Her very large, very plump breasts. Control yourself, man. He closed his eyes and tried not to think of the weight of them in his palms, the taste of her nipples on his tongue.

"Despite the fact that you're secreting enough pheromones to call a man from a mile away, I've yet to hear the words I need to proceed."

"What makes you think I'll ask you?"

He moved closer until he could almost rest his chin on her head, but he kept his arms by his side. As her breasts brushed his abdomen, his cock pulsated against her belly and she gasped in response.

"You're touching me," she whimpered, her voice breathless with desire.

"I have no control over my cock. It seeks to find comfort in you. It answers your body's call."

"My body's call?" Her body leaned into his. She rested her forehead against his chest and breathed her question against his skin. "What do you think my body is telling you?"

"The heat of your breasts scorch my skin, and peak at the thought of my lips tasting the sweet honey of your nipples while I fondle your beautiful, sensual breasts. Even as I speak, your pussy throbs as blood rushes to your clit, spreading damp heat between your legs. Tell me you want my hands to explore every inch of your body. My fingers to touch you, stroke you until you come in my hand. My tongue to taste you, my body to worship you, my—"

"No more talk." She pushed away from his chest to look into his eyes. "I want you, Chris. I want all those things you said."

"Thank the gods!"

He cupped her head, their lips melting together in a frenzied kiss as he lifted her. With her legs wrapped around his waist and his cock drenched in her arousal, he carried her to his bed. He would honor all his promises, make her come in ways she'd never believed possible, but for now...

****

No sooner had her back touched the smooth sheets of his bed, his hands were on her breasts. His tongue lapped at each breast in turn, until he chose one peak and drew it into his mouth, brushing her with his extended canine teeth. She arched her back as his fangs grazed the skin on her nipple and his tongue flicked out to lap up the droplets of blood. The sensible part of her warned herself to run. After all, he was a vampire. If he lost control, he may kill her, but dying in his arms would be worth it. He'd promised exquisite pleasure. Was this exquisite pain? If so, she liked it.

"More."

He took both her breasts in his hands, pushing them together, lapping and sucking on each nipple, taking a droplet of blood with each nip. As his mouth travelled down to her navel and kept going, she gasped. Her pelvis tilted in anticipation and her legs parted to give him full access.

"Yes. Sink your teeth into me."

Cupping her buttocks with his palms, he lifted her

bottom off the bed while he stared up at her face. His smile reminded her of the big, bad wolf from fairytales about to devour his prey, eat her all up. When his tongue flicked out to dampen his upper lip, she almost orgasmed and when he sunk his fangs into her clit, she screamed. "Oh. Fuck. Yes. Yes. Oh, yes."

Her knees held him firm, her hands gripped his hair close to his scalp and she thrust her hips hard against his mouth as she shuddered, again and again. Every cell in her body sang his praises. Every inch of her skin cried out for attention. Barely had his mouth broken contact with her pussy and she craved more. He seemed to anticipate her every need. His cock bobbed against her leg as he crawled along her body, kissing her abdomen, lapping the sweat in her navel and under her breasts. As he bit down on her left breast, she reached down and grabbed his shaft.

"Now. Fuck me, now."

He didn't hesitate, thrusting inside her. Filling her. Stretching her. She dug her nails into his buttocks, forcing him deeper inside her as she wrapped her legs around his waist to give him deeper penetration. As she arched her back, he suckled her breasts, squeezing them together as he groaned his approval.

"I knew they'd feel perfect in my hands."

She opened her eyes. "You think about me?"

"I think of nothing else." He sighed as his pelvis slammed into her with ever increasing speed. His hooded eyes closed and he groaned, his shuddering shaft vibrating inside her, sending another wave of pleasure through her body. She dug her fingernails into the flesh of his back and rode the wave, whimpering at its climax.

They lay together, her hands stroking his damp back. His body between her legs. Their hearts beating as one.

****

Evangeline checked the time on the bedside clock. 9:00 AM. Christoff would remain asleep for hours. She, on the other hand, was wide awake, and although the idea of lying beside his perfect body was appealing, she had work to do. Thank Christ she'd left her cell phone at home when they'd gone to the restaurant. Her mother would worry if she'd missed the weekly call. Before slinking out of bed, she leaned down and stroked the stray hair from his forehead before gently kissing his lips. He stirred, deepening the kiss as he pulled her down.

"Where are you going, min dyrebare? Come back to bed."

"I have to call my mother." She reluctantly pushed herself up and off the bed. "Besides, I thought you'd be in a hurry to get your treasure."

"I've already found my treasure." His smile made her weak at the knees until he sat up and raised an eyebrow. "Wait, you said mother?"

Trying hard not to start another fight, she grit her teeth and scowled. "Yes, I have a mother. I wasn't raised by wolves you know."

"Where is your mother? Does she travel with you?"

"She's not well." Should she trust him with the truth. "Actually, she's in hospice."

He reached out and took her hand, kissing it. "Her condition is terminal?"

Her head nodded of its own accord. Strange how that word made it all seem more real. Terminal. Dying. She sucked in a deep breath. *Not if I can help it.*

"Listen, Chris. I really need to talk to her, it's important." She slipped the dress over her head and checked under the bed.

"Looking for something?"

As she raised her head, he twirled the panties around on his index finger. "You can have this back, *if* you explain the urgency of your call."

Hands on hips, she challenged him. "Do you really think I'd be concerned about walking ten feet to my van, knickerless? Anyone living on the estate would be in their coffins."

He sat up, a bemused expression on his face. "Why do you humans insist on believing that vampires sleep in coffins. I have a perfectly nice, although half-empty, bed." He lifted back the sheet covering his erection and patted the mattress beside him. "Come, tell me why you are avoiding the subject of your mother."

Despite her almost instant arousal at the sight of his naked body, his last words dampened any flames of desire. How could she think of her own pleasure while her mother clung to life? She'd been careless with the medallion and almost lost any hope of saving the only person who mattered. Christoff had provided another opportunity to redeem herself and the price was worth every cent. Biting her bottom lip, she made a decision.

"I can't believe I'm going to tell you this." She lowered her chin, shook her head and continued. "I need money. Lots of it." Sliding onto the bed beside him, she gazed into his eyes, looking for compassion and finding it. "My mother has a rare blood disease. The doctors she's seen have no idea how to cure it." Biting back tears, she touched her fingers to her lips before continuing. "I've been trying to raise enough money to get a specialist, someone from Europe or wherever the hell blood specialists live."

When he silently stroked her hand, she broke down.

"No matter what you think of me, I'm not a bad person. I may scam the rich, but I don't sell my body.

The deal I made with you was out of desperation."

His expression changed. "Desperation? I don't understand. Why me? Why now?"

"Because." With a deep breath, she confessed something she could no longer deny, even to herself. "I wanted to do what you asked. I wanted *you*." She shook her head. "I know it's selfish, but I needed one night of pleasure. One moment's peace from the pain of knowing what's to come."

"Your mother?"

"She isn't expected to survive the month."

Evangeline shuddered as the words left her lips. Somehow, saying the words out loud made it seem more real. She wouldn't make enough money to save her mother. Time was up.

He crept up behind her, wrapping his arms around her, holding her, as he whispered into her ear. "Then your mother shall have the best doctors and medical attention money can buy."

When Evangeline turned around and opened her mouth to speak, he silenced her with a finger to her lips.

"Consider this a gift. There will be no more talk of selling your body. It cheapens our love."

Love? Suddenly the strength left her legs and she wobbled in his arms. "What did you say?"

"I told you the money would be a gift."

"No, the other thing."

One side of his mouth curled. "I said I wanted no more talk of selling yourself."

She pushed him away with a shove to his naked chest and raised her left eyebrow when she realized. "You bastard. You're teasing me."

"Perhaps, perhaps not." Despite his taunt, he chuckled.

"You love me?"

"From the moment I saw you."

"But I thought you wanted to punish me for robbing those people?"

"Ah, so you admit to your deceptions."

"You mean this." She drew her right arm across her body and with a sideways flick of her hand, threw him onto the bed. His shocked expression brought a smile to her face. "If you want to play games, I'm happy to oblige."

As she knelt on the end of his bed and crawled towards him, she used her telekinetic powers to hold him down, motionless except for the throbbing of his cock.

"Are you going to punish me?" His words cracked, sounding more like a request than a question. She had him right where she wanted him. Her smile widened as she straddled his hips, lifting her dress to remind him her underwear lay somewhere on the floor. He groaned as she pressed forward, pinning his cock against his abdomen as she rubbed her clit the length of his impressive erection.

"Would you *like* me to punish you?"

His eyes widened, and his mouth curled in a grin as wide as his face as he nodded.

However, she wasn't finished with him yet.

"I've told you my story." She leaned closer, her hair brushing his neck, her breath on his chest. "Tell me how you became a vampire."

His sharp intake of breath surprised her. She leaned back to study his face. Why was he so reluctant to tell her? So far, he'd been brutally honest with every answer, every question. Why was this time so different?

"My story may not be to your liking." He averted her gaze, looking down to the side. "I am not proud of the things I did leading to my demise. I doubt you would think of me the same way once you hear the truth."

She sat back on the bed, her bottom still between his legs and crossed her arms. "When we first met, you accused me of being a whore, but you still wanted me. Let me be the judge. I'm pretty open-minded."

"Very well."

****

Christoff sucked in a deep breath and closed his eyes. Would she run from him after hearing his confession? Would the truth set him free or bind him in the chains of loneliness forever?

"At the age of thirty, I found myself left behind in a Danish seaside village after my shipmates had sailed without me. We had attacked the village, expecting an easy victory, but we were wrong. The townspeople fought bravely and drove us back to the ship. I fell and broke my leg and was left behind."

"No honor amongst pirates?"

"I guess that was what we were, however, the common name for my people was Vikings."

"No shit? Vikings?"

"Shall I continue?"

"A fire had broken out, much like the one from the restaurant. I would prefer to think that they couldn't find me. Being intentionally left sounds much worse. Regardless of the reason, I found myself at the mercy of the villagers. One young lass, the chief's daughter, took a fancy to me. With all the younger men married, she had been expected to marry a much older man, so she convinced her father that I was a better option."

Lines crinkled Evangeline's forehead. "How old was she?"

"Fifteen." He stopped her next words with an extended palm. "I realize the age difference between us is abhorrent in this century, but it was common practice back then. Besides, the other candidates for husband were in their fifties and I was given a choice. The chapel or the gallows."

"So, you married her?"

He nodded, ashamed that his words stole the sparkle from her eyes.

"Did you love her?"

"I loved her, but I was not *in love* with her. I became fond of her. She tried to be the perfect wife in every way, but in the bed chamber, she acted like the child she was. At no stage of our marriage did she ever disrobe in front of me and she always wore a long, flannel nightgown to bed to cover her body while making love."

"That must have sucked for you."

"It wasn't ideal, especially after experiencing the pleasures of the flesh at many ports—"

"I think you can skip that part."

Her expression warned him to do just that.

"How did you become a vampire?"

"After your reaction to my last confession, I think, perhaps, I shouldn't go into details."

Her nose crinkled, and her huge eyes narrowed with her frown.

"Fine. During my first winter in the village, a woman arrived by sea in a small vessel. She soon fell afoul of the gossip, especially as she was unescorted and preferred to sleep the days away on board her boat. At first, I pitied her as I, too, was not the most welcome of newcomers, but," he eased back up the bedhead, trying to subtly remove his genitals from within her reach, "she was the most sensual being I had ever laid eyes on. Her face and body as smooth as marble. Her—"

"I get the picture." Evangeline cleared her voice. "She seduced you and you left town with her."

"Yes, she seduced me." He stared into her eyes.

Would she understand why he did what he did? Why he became the man who even other vampires feared? "I did not leave willingly."

"I'm sure every cheating asshole tells the same sob story." She slipped her legs over his and onto the floor. Before she had a chance to rise from the bed, he reached out and snagged her wrist.

"Somebody betrayed you?"

"Not just me." She kept her back to him as she added, "my worthless piece of shit of a father left us when I was a young girl. Since then, I seem to attract men just like him."

"I will never hurt you, min dyrebare. Nor will I leave you."

She spun around to face him. "How can I trust you? You cheated on your wife and left her. How do I know you won't do that to me?"

He swung his legs over the side of the bed and rose to hold her. *A man could get lost in those doe eyes.* "I had no choice but to leave. The sex was more than intense, it became violent." She tried to pull away from him, but he forced her to listen. He needed her to understand.

"She tore at my clothes, bruised my body, bit into my skin. I felt the sting as her fangs punctured my flesh and tried to push her away. Before I had time to comprehend what she was, I felt my body dying. When she slashed her wrist with her teeth and dripped her own blood into my mouth, I had no strength to fight her. I awoke onboard her boat, craving human blood."

Evangeline's eyes widened. "Tell me you didn't kill your wife."

He shook his head. "The woman tried to coerce me into it, but I refused. Once again, I was forced to make a choice. Kill my wife or leave the village forever.

We set sail the same day."

"How long did you stay with the vampire?"

"We parted company at the first port. She wanted a partner in crime. I wanted to make my death permanent. Neither of us would accept a compromise."

She slipped her arms around him, her head resting on his chest, her body tantalizingly warm. "I'm glad you didn't off yourself."

"Off myself? Oh, you mean kill myself? Yes, I'm glad, too. Especially now."

"What happened to make you change your mind?" Her heart fluttered against his rib cage. Was she concerned he may have found another woman?

"I found a reason for living. While I detested the idea of killing innocents, punishing evil doers soon became a source of nourishment, plus a calling for me. Humans came to think of me as Karma. Retribution for their sins. Neither are vampires immune to my swift justice. I am known to them as the enforcer as I am called upon to destroy those who still kill humans."

"Don't all vampires eat humans?" she breathed against his chest sending a wave of heat through his body.

"This type of behavior is no longer acceptable. Blood banks supply our nourishment. Some humans allow vampires to take small amounts of blood during intercourse."

She lifted her head, pushing slightly away to look up into his eyes.

"Intercourse? Wow, Chris. Could you be any more proper?"

Was that a question or an insult? "What would you have me say?"

She waved off his question. "Never mind. I want to know more about this woman. Did you ever see her again?"

****

Christoff nodded his head. "After me, she went on to create many other vampires, both male and female. Some—like David, the man who this property belongs to—she left without proper instruction as to how to remain undetected. Her carelessness gained her notoriety and the council of vampires sent me to hunt and kill her."

"I don't understand," Evangeline sat back down onto the edge of the bed, "I've watched enough vampire movies to know that, if you kill the sire, all the fledglings die. Why aren't you and this David, dead?"

"Myths." He told her, his naked body close, his burgeoning arousal inches from her face.

She turned her head. "For fuck's sake. Will you put some pants on?"

His eyes twinkled with mischief. "Are you sure that's what you want?"

"Very sure." How could she concentrate on the story while her hands itched to touch him?

With a shrug, he turned his back and walked casually towards the dresser. She suspected that the sway of his tight behind was a deliberate attempt to seduce her. She closed her eyes and tried to think of other things. Unfortunately, the first thought that came to mind was his job. He said that he'd been tracking her for weeks. Was she to suffer the same fate as the female vampire? Was it his intention to punish her? By the time he'd dressed, her heart was beating a mile a minute and she could barely catch her breath.

"Listen, Chris. Whatever you plan on doing to me, please don't punish my mother for my mistakes. She thinks I sell cosmetics door to door to help with the hospice bills. There isn't a bad bone in her body."

"Calm down." He held her shoulders as he stared

into her eyes. His expression puzzled her. Why did he look so concerned? "I have no intention of hurting you or your mother."

Her heart wanted to believe him. Needed to believe him. Experience reminded her that you don't always get what you want.

"But you tracked me, and you keep me captive on this property. What *do* you plan on doing with me?"

"I can think of many things," his fingers lightly stroked the bare skin on her arms, "and none include hurting you."

"Stop that." She brushed his hands away, afraid that he'd stop her from asking the inevitable question. "Did the vampire council send you to kill me?"

He frowned his surprise. "No. Why would they? The council does not concern itself with human behavior."

"But—"

"Dark forces drew me to this town. Your telekinesis directed me to you. I've dealt with an energy such as yours before. At first, I was curious as to how you deceived the homeowners and after watching you, I became aware of a force greater than your own. Someone or something is trying to connect with you. It was no accident finding the medallion. It called to you."

She let out the breath she'd unknowingly held. "Dark forces? Am I that dark force?"

"I will not lie to you," he took her hands in his. Bile rose in her throat. *This can't be good.* "I do sense evil inside you. Not in your deeds or thoughts, but in your DNA."

"How could you possibly know what's in my DNA?"

He lowered his chin, looked up at her from under his lashes and licked his lips.

For a moment, she wondered what he meant, then, the penny dropped. A flood of blood rushed to her crotch as she remembered the intense pleasure when he sank his fangs into her arousal. She bit her bottom lip as her cheeks flushed with heat.

"Never mind." So, somewhere in her gene pool, was an evil doer. But who? Was it her fate to become a serial killer or something equally evil? Could she do anything to prevent it? A thought crossed her mind. Maybe the thief had done her a favor after all. "The medallion is gone. That means it won't affect me, right?"

"I am concerned." He scratched the back of his head and looked down at the floor. "You said that you opened the locket. Normally, talismans are sealed by magic. If it was easy for you to open—"

"You had me worried for a minute." She sighed with relief. "It wasn't easy to open. There was no catch. I had to pry it open with a knife." She held out her hand. "Look. The damned point went through my palm. I bled like a pig."

He closed his eyes, shaking his head as he asked, "Did you bleed onto the locket?"

"Aha. I bled everywhere. When I dropped it to grab paper towels, the locket broke open and a little piece of metal fell out."

His grip on her arms tightened. "You must give me the scroll. Do not open it under any circumstances, do you hear me? Bring it to me, now."

"All right, already." She rose to her feet and shot him her best resting bitch face look before heading towards the door. *Geez, talk about being melodramatic.* She'd been on her way to collect it earlier. It was his fault she didn't bring it to him already. *Maybe I should take my time getting back?* She turned her head to look back. If he'd been a cartoon character, there'd be steam coming out of his ears. *On second thought, maybe I should hurry.*

****

When she reached the van, she closed her eyes. *Please let this be a bad dream. Please wake up.* But when she opened them, the door to her caravan still hung off its hinges.

"No." She screamed aloud as she leapt the steps into her home. Drawers lay broken on the ground, the contents spilled everywhere. Cabinet doors didn't fare any better than the front door, all torn from their hinges. Who would do this? The curtain dividing her bedroom from the living area had been pulled away from the rod, giving her clear view into her wardrobe where the safe door lay open.

Her breath caught when she gazed into the empty safe. She fell to the floor, sobbing until the smell of burning flesh forced her to raise her head.

"The scroll?"

She watched in horror and then surprise as Christoff's blistered skin healed before her eyes as he sheltered in the darkest corner of her room. His face and hands turned from red to a deep pink.

"Gone." She grabbed fistfuls of her hair and tugged. *Please wake up.* It didn't work. "Everything's gone. The scroll, the money for Mom, my phone. Everything."

"We can't stay here."

His statement puzzled her. "Why not? Do you think they're still here?" She scanned the room. "Will they come back?"

He gnashed his teeth. "All of those things are possible, but my concern is that I won't be in a position to protect you if I combust." He reached for the quilt and snatched it off her bed. "May I borrow this?"

Before she had a chance to agree, he'd thrown the

covering over his head and cocooned himself inside.

"Come on," she snagged his arm and dragged him to the entrance of the van, "you look like a taco and smell like Southern fried chicken. Suddenly I'm hungry."

When they entered his darkened cottage, he threw off the covering. "Seriously, you have an appetite after seeing your home ransacked?"

"I'm a stress eater." She told him as she flopped down onto his couch. "Things like having my life savings stolen and my stuff destroyed have that effect on me."

The tension in the room was palpable. What would he do to her? Would he blame her for the theft of the scroll? As her stomach twisted in knots, he paced the kitchen, pulling at his hair and muttering to himself before suddenly turning his attention back to her.

"I think it's best you live with me. At least until your van is repaired."

Well, that was unexpected. "Thanks." What choice did she have? All her savings were in that safe and, along with that, her only hope of making enough money to help her mother.

He dropped to one knee in front of her and took both her hands in his. "Don't worry about the money. Your mother will receive all the help she needs. I personally guarantee it."

Something akin to joy set her heart to flutter. "Really? Do you mean it?"

He placed his hand to his heart. "My word is my bond."

As she threw herself into his arms, he toppled backwards, taking her down with him while she rained kisses on his cheeks. "I'm going to thank you so hard you'll be begging me for mercy."

A grin curled his mouth at the corners, but he held her at arms' length. "I very much look forward to that, but first, I need to make a few calls."

"Huh." She sat back, positioning herself over his crotch as she crossed her arms and pouted. "What's more important than my gratitude?"

He pulled her down for a kiss that left her weak at the knees and desperate for more. When he eased her off his lap and rose, lifting her with him, his words made her love him even more.

"I have contacts in Europe. The type of specialists you mentioned might be able to help your mother. I want to call them and start the ball rolling."

Chapter Six

Evangeline yawned and stretched out her arms above her head. "I feel like I've slept for a week. What time is it?"

"It's after 4:00 PM."

"You're shitting me. I rarely nap in the afternoon." Her left eye winked suggestively. "You must have worn me out." She ran her fingers through the masses of unruly curls and yawned again. "Who was that on the phone?"

"Nothing to worry about, go back to sleep." He reached down to tuck her in, but she stopped him with a slap to his hand.

"You've always been brutally honest with me. Don't start lying to me now."

He plonked down onto the bed beside her. "That was Palmer. While you slept, he swept your home for fingerprints."

She sat up in bed, a hopeful expression on her face. "Do they have any leads?"

He shook his head, wondering how much he should tell her.

"Whoever broke in wore gloves." That was the truth. Omitting to tell her that Anna had a vision wasn't exactly a lie. Or was it?

Her downcast expression troubled him. If *that* news upset her, how could he tell her about the earlier phone conversation?

"What is it you're not telling me?" Her voice rose in pitch. "Is it about the scroll? Have you changed your mind about loaning me the money?"

"The money would have been a gift, not a loan." A heaviness weighed down on his chest. A sensation he had long forgotten. It pained him to know the grief his words would cause her.

"Would have? You're not going to give me the money?" she sat up in the bed, her breasts heaving under the thin fabric of the shirt he'd earlier discarded to the floor. "Look, Chris. I'm sorry that I didn't hide the scroll well enough to fool the thieves. Please, I need that money. My mother –"

"The money will not help your mother now."

Her beautiful dark eyes widened, and she continued to shake her head while he told her what he feared would break her heart.

"I called the hospice earlier to make the necessary arrangements for your mother's care. They'd been trying to call you."

"No." she sobbed, holding her hands over her ears. "I won't listen to this. I don't want to hear this." Tears spilled down her cheeks. "She's getting better. We're going to find a cure."

He leaned towards her and she collapsed into his arms. Her tears soaked his shirt as he held her tight to his chest. "The doctor said she died peacefully in her sleep."

"I don't believe you." Her wails reverberated through his chest cavity. "They wouldn't give you that information."

"I told them I was your husband." He felt her body stiffen in his arms. "There was nothing to be done for her." He'd already called every blood specialist in the world. Evangeline's doctor had emailed him the case files. No one had seen anything like her disease. No amount of money would have changed that.

He lifted her chin with his index finger, so he could be sure she heard his words. "There is no easy way to tell you this, min dyrebare. Your mother's blood had been tainted with demon blood."

"Demon blood?" Lines creased her forehead as she wiped her nose with the back of her hand. "How would she have Demon blood in her veins and, why do you keep calling me a bear? Don't you think that's a shitty thing to say considering what you just told me? Don't you even have a heart?" Her cheeks flushed with color and despite her snarl, she sniffed back a sob.

Try as he might, he couldn't contain his smile. "I would sooner cut out my tongue than call you anything derogative. The English translation for min dyrebare, is *my precious*. You have made me your Gollum. I cannot part with you, no matter what it costs me."

Her back stiffened. "How the fuck do you expect me to respond to that?"

Her words surprised him. Was she not happy to hear that he loved her?

"I don't understand your anger. Is it because you are grieving for your mother?" That must be it. He'd confessed his love too soon.

She scooted out of bed, shaking her head. "You tell me I'm precious and insult me in the same breath. I've seen the movie, I know that the ring is evil and must be destroyed. Where do you get off saying that you can't part with me, no matter what it costs you? Who says I want to be with you anyway?"

The color in her cheeks deepened to a shade of mulberry and her body began to shake violently as she stood by the bed. He expected her to rant or, at the very least, use her power to throw something at him. When she opened her mouth to speak, he braced himself for a verbal attack. Her actions took him by surprise.

A high-pitched scream tore from her lips as her face twisted into a mask of pain. She fell to the floor, convulsing. Heat radiated from her skin, blisters formed on her flesh. The borrowed shirt, now saturated in sweat, clung to her body. Wide eyes stared up at him, begging him to do something to stop the pain. He reached down and, ignoring the heat that scorched his own body, carried her to the bathtub. Gently, he lay her down, supporting her head as he turned the cold water to full capacity. Steam rose from her body. The water bubbled as the heat from her skin brought it to a boil. Her scream warned him to remove her from the bath, so he carried her back to the bed, desperately trying to think of another plan.

Rushing to the refrigerator, he poured ice cubes into a clean, wet tea towel and returned to place it on her skin. Within seconds, the ice melted, and the cloth became hot to touch. Helplessly, he sat on the edge of the bed and watched as her lips first became parched then began to crack and swell. The whites of her eyes deepened to pale pink and, when the irises rolled back, his heart physically ached.

"Hold on, my love. Fight this. Don't leave me."

She closed her eyes for a few minutes and, when she opened them, the tinge of blood had begun to fade. Her breathing steadied and she rewarded him with a weak smile.

"I think. Its. Going. Away," she sighed as her body relaxed.

He took her hand and kissed it. "I thought I was going to lose you."

"Me, too." She struggled to a sitting position as he placed pillows behind her shoulders. "I guess what they say about 'only the good die young' must be right."

"This is no laughing matter." He warned. "Something was trying to kill you."

"No." She looked down at her lap. "Something was trying to *contact* me."

"Surely not your mother?" From what Evangeline had told him, her mother would never inflict such harm on her only child. Or could she? He'd been undead, so long. Were humans really that heartless?

Evangeline shook her head. "I don't know how to explain it. I felt power. Real power." She raised her head to look at him. "I saw the medallion and … it spoke to me."

"I blame myself." Christoff let out a sigh as he stroked a damp curl from her face. "I should have forced you to give me the medallion *before* we went to dinner."

She shrugged her shoulders. "If I'd had my way, I would have tricked you out of it anyway. If you remember, I took the scroll hoping to convince you to pay more."

"It would have worked." He pinched her chin between his thumb and index finger, pulling her face in for a kiss. "You've put a spell on me, my precious."

She caught his bottom lip in her teeth and tugged. "Back at ya, Gollum. But why would the medallion want me?"

In his heart, he already knew the answer, but he hoped to be wrong. "Describe the medallion to me. I want to know every detail."

Her forehead creased. "I don't understand. Haven't you seen the medallion?"

"I *felt* its presence." He rose from the bed and turned his back to her. "I sensed the evil connected to it and wished to destroy it before—"

"Before some idiot unleashed its power."

"What's done is done." He turned back. "Now, if you please, describe it to me."

She closed her eyes, tilting her chin up as her mouth twisted at the side. "Okay. Well, the first thing I noticed about it was the heat it gave off." Her jaw clenched as she opened her eyes. "I should have taken that as a warning, right?" she shook her head. "All I could see was dollar signs. I needed the money so badly. I didn't think—"

He sat beside her and held her shoulders. "That heat you felt was the power. You were already under its enchantment, but I need you to concentrate. Tell me everything you remember."

With a nod, she continued. "I remember a wolf with bared teeth. Not the pretty type you normally see in tattoos and paintings, this one looked angry, as if he wanted to bite your face off. There was a design … no, two different designs around him." She looked up at him. "I thought this was a bit strange because one was like a snake without a head or a tail, while the other was geometrical. They didn't match."

Bile churned in the pit of his stomach. "The geometric design. Could it have been a letter? Perhaps the initial W?"

"Yes, maybe. Either W or M. I remember thinking that it looked like an optical illusion."

"And the wolf, was it inside a circle?"

She scratched her head and her lips moved wordlessly as she seemed to count. "Yes, three circles. Two surrounding the patterns. One around the top of the head, like a halo."

"Not a halo, a moon." There was no longer any doubt. Lupescu was back.

"You've seen it? I thought you said—"

"I've seen the design, not the medallion." His hands dropped from her shoulders and hung limp by his sides. "What you said earlier about not looking like a regular tattoo. That's because its worn by cult members who would kill you in a heartbeat if their leader instructed them. You've heard of Charles Manson?"

She nodded, the color draining from her cheeks. "Was *he* their leader?"

"This man would make Manson and his followers look like amateurs." And now he was back and worse still, trying to contact Evangeline. "I've killed him once, but now that Lupescu is stronger, I'm … what's the matter?"

****

"You're shitting me." Evangeline could literally feel the color drain from her cheeks. Moments ago, they'd burned with heat and now … now they felt as cold as ice. "You're saying that the monster who's messing with my head is Lupescu? Mánagarmr Lupescu?"

Christoff's expression was enough to convince her that he wasn't kidding.

"You know who he is?"

Her heart slammed against her chest, robbing her of breath. She held out her palm, hoping for time to regain her breath before answering.

"He's … my father." She held her palms to her temples as the pounding rose from her chest to her head. Had her father disappeared because he wanted to leave or because Christoff killed him? How different would she have been if she hadn't been forced into a life of crime? She stared into the face of her father's killer and tried to hate him, but it was no use. She knew in her heart, he'd probably done what needed to be done.

"Lupescu was no longer a man when I executed him. He'd made a pact with a demon in exchange for supernatural abilities, but the demon's blood proved too powerful, even for a mage as strong as your father. It consumed him. Poisoned his mind." He reached for her and held her by her forearms. "This won't be easy for you to hear."

She laughed an uneasy giggle. Easy? In one morning she'd lost a mother and gained a monster for a father. Her body had been tortured, almost to death. What else could he say to hurt her? Except…

"Oh, god. You're saying that I'm a combination of demon and mage?"

"There is more." He looked down at his feet and she knew instantly what his next words would be.

There was no way she could hear those words from someone else, especially him. She reached her hand to grab hold of the edge of the bed as the strength left her body. "I poisoned my mother?"

He ran his fingers through his hair and she realized by his expression that he was trying to find a kind way to continue. The notion surprised her. Maybe he really did care for her, after all? Hopefully, he'd get over it.

"Don't hold back now, Chris." She swung her legs over the side of the thick mattress and planted her feet firmly on the plush carpet. "Just say it. Dad's demon sperm produced me and as I grew in her belly, my diseased blood slowly began to kill her."

His shoulders drooped, but he said nothing.

"You *can't* lie, can you?" She could feel the corners of her mouth curl into a bitter smile as she forced down the sob that caught in her throat. "I have to go."

He snagged her wrist as she tried to rush past. "Wait. We should discuss this."

"I'm not ready to talk about it." With a tug, she pulled free of his grip, but he followed her to the door.

"Stay. In a couple of hours, it will be dark. I'll take you anywhere you want to go."

"I. Said. No." She spun on her heel and thrust out her palm, sending him sailing back into the bedroom. He raised himself to a sitting position against the wall, but made no attempt to stand. His wounded expression broke her heart.

As she slammed the door behind her, she hoped

that he would forgive her for what she had done and, also, what she was about to do.

****

Heads turned as she marched up to the bar, plonked her barely covered butt on the stool and ordered a Jack and Coke. Hours earlier, she'd been naked in Christoff's bed, but somehow, she felt more exposed, more vulnerable, in the tiny shorts and low-cut shirt she'd deliberately chosen to wear. If her plan worked, she'd be contacted by her father's followers. If not, at the very least, she hoped she could con someone into shouting a few drinks. The twenty dollars she'd stashed away in a cookie jar would not be enough to drown the pain. Goddamned minions. If only they'd taken the medallion and left the money in the safe.

"You look lonely."

The middle-aged man's breath stank of stale beer. He sat on the stool beside her. "Buy you a drink, honey."

"Sure, why not?" she forced a smile and motioned to the bartender for another Jack and Coke while pretending not to notice the attention her breasts were getting from her drinking companion. She raised her glass. "Bottoms up."

"Your choice, darlin." He ran a dirty, calloused palm up her thigh, sending a shudder through her body.

She pushed the hand away and shook her head. "It wasn't an offer."

"But I bought you a drink?"

He genuinely looked surprised by her response. Did he really think that she would put out for the price of one drink? Is that the way everyone saw her? She downed the whiskey in one gulp, ignoring the mutterings of the man as he shuffled away, then ordered a straight Jack. No point watering it down. Time to get well and truly drunk.

"My friend here says you owe him something."

Blazing eyes stared down at her. This man appeared to be younger than the other. Maybe thirty something? His t-shirt strained over his broad chest and shoulders as he puffed out his pecs.

"Go away." She shooed him with a flick of her wrist as she turned her attention back to her fourth drink of the evening. "I'm busy."

He slapped the drink from her hand, the glass shattered on the counter and the noisy room suddenly became silent. Adrenaline jump-started her nerves. Her body, although feeling the effects of the alcohol, prepared for an attack.

"Outside, bitch. I'm gonna show you what happens to cock teasers in my town." He grabbed his crotch. "And then, I think I'll let you suck my dick."

"Pass." She tilted her head in the direction of the older guy. "I wouldn't put my mouth where your boyfriend has been."

The backhand took her by surprise, knocking her off the stool. She looked around the room, losing any hope for support as the bar cleared of everyone, except her attacker and two of his companions. Holding her jaw, she scooted along on her bottom until her back hit the wall. Two of the men lifted her to her feet and held her under the arms as the bully tugged at the knot holding the ends of her shirt tied provocatively under her breasts. She'd been warned this day would come, but why today? Hadn't she suffered enough?

Something inside her stirred, urging her to fight. No. Not fight, kill. Breathing in short, strong bursts, she felt her body temperature rise, her heartbeat gain momentum, every muscle in her body swell and tighten. By the time the thug had loosened the knot and opened her shirt to expose her bra, she'd turned the fear to rage. When he looked up triumphantly, the stupid smile on his face soon dissolved.

"What the fuck!"

"What is it?" The man to her right loosened his grip on her arm and she took the opportunity to rip it from his grasp and wrap her fingers around the throat of her attacker, lifting him off the ground.

When the others tried to assist, she sent them flying, using the power of her mind. They hit the ground running, leaving their comrade behind.

"Your eyes." He gasped as she tightened her grip, her fingernails digging into his flesh.

She turned her head to face the mirrored backsplash behind the bar. It took a few seconds for her mind to register that the purple eyes staring back at her were her own.

"Please."

"What did you say?"

The man dangling at the end of her outstretched arm gasped. His eyes bulged. Blood vessels burst, staining the whites of his eyes with forked red lines. Thick veins protruded on his forehead and temples and she could feel his pulse slow beneath her finger and thumb as she simultaneously pressed down on both his carotid arteries. Power surged through her veins and she liked everything about it. The strength, the electricity, the control. This low-life and his friends had planned to gang rape her. Now look at him, pissing his pants with fear as she choked the life out of him. How easy would it be to snap his neck? She'd be doing the town a favor.

"This isn't you."

"You don't know me." She told him without turning around. "You don't know what this bastard was going to do to me."

"I'm sure that, one day, he'll get what he deserves, but not today. Not at your hand."

In the blink of an eye, he was by her side. His hands at her wrist, gently tugging at her fingers. "If you do this, there's no coming back."

"I don't care." Tears burned behind her eyes. "I'm numb, Chris. I need to feel something, anything." She turned her head to face him, her cheeks damp with tears. "I can't live with the knowledge my mother died because of me."

"This isn't the way." His breath feathered against her neck and she felt her resolve melt away.

The man dropped to the floor, landing in the pool of urine his fear had created. Evangeline slumped into Christoff's arms. He scooped her up and carried her to the door as she peeked over his shoulder.

"Is he?"

"No."

"Good." She said aloud, but the voice in her head roared. *You should have finished him. He deserved to die.* With her head resting on Christoff's muscled shoulder, she closed her eyes and tried to force the murderous thoughts from her mind. No use. Instead, she redirected her rage to where it belonged. To the monster who'd caused her the most pain. Oh, she'd have her revenge. She'd make him pay for what he'd done to her, and her mother. This was going to be a father/daughter reunion to remember, except, he wouldn't live to regret it.

Chapter Seven

"Your apocalypse has started."

"Is that how you greet all your guests at the door?" Christoff growled as he waited for the unnecessary invitation to cross the threshold.

Terry motioned for them to enter his home and followed them into the living room.

"A friend from my old precinct phoned me. There was a disturbance at the local pub last night. Some superwoman beat up an innocent guy and left him for dead. There's an all-points bulletin out for her."

"Oh, great." Evangeline mumbled under her breath.

"You?" Terry lifted an eyebrow as his gaze drifted from Evangeline to Christoff.

"It wasn't her fault." He explained. "And the man she choked wasn't innocent."

"I expected as much." Terry pointed to the settee and sat on the chair facing them. "He has a reputation for hurting women. We haven't been able to pin anything on him yet as the witnesses always change their mind at the last minute."

"I believe that he'll think twice next time." Evangeline snickered. After a quick glance at Terry, she bit her lip and looked down at her feet.

"I will be watching him." Christoff informed him. Despite his orders to protect humans, he had made more than a few predators disappear over the years. "His next attack will be his last."

"As a former officer of the law, I'm going to pretend I didn't hear that." Terry looked up to the ceiling, his lips formed a tight line. "We didn't even discuss him."

"But we did discuss him." Christoff protested. "How could you forget so quickly? Are you unwell?"

Terry's shoulders dropped, and he sighed as he tilted his head in Evangeline's direction. "Do you believe this guy?"

"He's a hard nut to crack."

"Hey! No picking on the big guy." Susie entered the room in response to his telepathic message. Their words were lost on him. He needed a translator.

Terry motioned for her to sit in his lap where he wrapped his arms around her belly. Christoff felt the sting of jealousy. The experience surprised him. Enforcing the vampire law was all he'd ever cared about but now... Now he envied his friends and the family they had created. Susie glowed with joy despite the morning sickness that often plagued her. Their telepathic connection gave him more of an insight into her emotions than she realized. The baby was healing her psychological wounds. She smiled to Evangeline.

"Maybe you could teach me how to defend myself. After the baby arrives, of course."

Evangeline forced a smile. "I would if I could. The entire thing is a blur. He and his thugs threatened to rape me. Next thing I knew, he was dangling in the air with my fingers around his throat, pissing down his pants."

Susie's eyes opened wide and she took Christoff by surprise when she burst out laughing.

"I'm sorry," she held her hand to her mouth, but the giggles kept escaping. "I know I shouldn't laugh, but your description was so vivid." She turned to face Christoff. "I like her. I think we're going to become good friends."

Susie's words gave him hope for Evangeline's salvation. A friend like Susie might be just what she needed. Someone with shared experiences. But would she object to him disclosing the traumas of her past? Was she ready for a stranger to know her story? She instantly answered his extrasensory question with a yes. *You have my blessing to tell her anything that might help her get through this.*

He smiled and nodded his thanks. Evangeline raised an eyebrow.

"I'll explain in the car on the way home," he whispered, close to her ear.

"Okay, let's get this party started." Terry lifted his wife and put her in his vacated seat. "Drinks?"

"Party? I thought we were here to discuss the impending danger?" Had he missed something?

Evangeline held her palm to her forehead, shook her head and then raised her chin to face Terry. "I think I'll have one of those drinks."

"Iced tea coming up." He smiled to the guests and headed to the kitchen.

Evangeline frowned and whispered to Christoff, "Iced tea? I thought he meant real drinks?"

When Terry returned, carrying a tray of glasses and a jug of herbal tea, he half smiled his apology. "Susie insists that, if she can't drink alcohol, no one in this house can."

"Seems fair." Evangeline accepted her drink and took a sip before placing the glass on the coffee table. "Let's cut to the chase. My father is back in town and I plan to kill him before he causes any trouble. Who's with me?"

"Back up a bit." Terry squeezed in beside Susie. "This is a human problem?"

Christoff stopped Evangeline with an extended palm, before she could answer. There was more to the story than even she understood. Perhaps hearing it in a friendly environment might lessen the shock.

"Mánagarmr Lupescu was once a man. He made a Faustian pact with a demon to make him a powerful mage. As you know, Demons are not the most honorable of supernatural beings and demanded more than the usual pound of flesh. It entered his body to impregnate Evangeline's mother. Her human body was not strong enough to tolerate the demon's blood and after the birth, she became ill." He turned to Evangeline and thread his fingers through hers. "She lost her fight yesterday."

"Oh, no." Susie leapt from her husband's lap and almost threw herself at her new friend. "I'm so sorry. If there's ever anything I can do to help. A shoulder to cry on—"

Evangeline bristled. "Thanks, but I'm fine." She looked down at her feet while Susie returned to her seat. Christoff continued his story.

"When Evangeline was approximately six years old, I was instructed to destroy Lupescu. The demon had almost completely taken over his body, so he was no longer considered to be human. We expected his followers to disband after the mage's death, but we were wrong. Recent information has come to light." He reached into his pocket, pulled out a photograph and passed it around. When it reached Evangeline, he asked, "Is this what you saw on the locket?"

She nodded her head. "Is this a tattoo?"

He addressed his answer to the room. "This photograph was taken off a body in the morgue after the police shot him three months ago. He was killed while attempting to sacrifice a child."

"A child?" Susie almost screeched.

"The child was unharmed. Unfortunately, the other cult members escaped."

"I remember that case." Terry scratched his head.

"There was a medallion involved. We found it around the kid's neck. I don't know what happened to it."

"I do." Evangeline told him. "Some idiot opened it."

"Who would do a dumb ass thing ... oh."

"Yep. That would be me."

Christoff explained how Evangeline's blood was the key to open the locket. He told them about the metal scroll. "Have you ever heard of a curse tablet?" He asked.

Susie raised her hand. "I have. I remember learning about it at college. If you wanted someone to pay for an injustice, you would scratch or engrave a curse onto a piece of lead and hide it under their house. Some curse tablets were found in cemeteries or wells."

Evangeline shrugged her shoulders. "I don't get it. How does that work?"

"The curse would be addressed to a demon who would punish the person named on the scroll."

"Okay, I get the curse tablet and the blood thing." Terry scratched his head as he furrowed his brows. "But what I don't get is, who is the scroll cursing?"

"I believe that would be me." It was only a matter of time before someone cursed him. His enemies numbered in the hundreds, maybe thousands. Sooner or later, his number would be up, but why now? Was fate really cruel enough to deny him one moment's happiness?

All eyes turned to Christoff, but it was Evangeline who spoke first.

"You? Oh, shit. That's why the charm was so important to you." She leaned forward, supporting her forehead with her hands. "You're right about me. I'm no good. If I wasn't so selfish, you'd have the medallion and none of us would be in this mess." She raised her head, tears in her eyes as she asked him, "I've as good as killed you, haven't I?"

"I think that boat sailed a while back." Terry interjected. He received an elbow to his mid-section from Susie for his insensitivity.

"What do you think they're planning?" Susie asked Christoff. Her troubled expression warmed his cold heart. The little one was concerned for him.

"True death. Possibly after days of torture."

Evangeline's gasp synchronized with Susie's. Only Terry seemed unfazed.

"Oh, come on. You couldn't possibly believe that a bunch of hooded goths could take down big guy here? He'll obliterate them." He held his hand out to Christoff for a fist bump and received a frown for his troubles.

Evangeline's spirits seemed to lift. She raised her head, her eyes twinkled with hope as she smiled at him. Christoff didn't have the heart to explain his handicap, but Susie had no hesitation.

"He can't hurt a human. If he harms or, heaven forbid, kills one. The vampire council will execute him."

"Then … I'll do it. I'll kill them. It's all my fault anyway."

"I can't let you do that, min dyrebare. For many reasons."

Evangeline crossed her arms and shot him a scowl. "Name one."

"You forget the reason I found you in the first place. My task is to hunt evil doers and punish them."

She rose to her feet and stared down at him. Her pained expression cut him to the quick. Once again, his honesty had hurt her. If only he could learn to lie like other men.

"I can't believe you. You would kill me for protecting you?"

"It would pain me to do so, but yes."

"Well, fuck you." She stormed to the door. "Maybe I should just let them have you."

In an instant, he blocked her path. "I can't change who I am."

She glared into his eyes. Her lips tantalizingly close, but he dared not kiss her. Even *he* knew it would be a bad idea.

"Neither can I."

"Both of you. Sit down and let's discuss this." Susie called to them from her seat.

"There's nothing to discuss." Evangeline told her, without shifting her gaze from Christoff's face. "The party's over."

"I disagree." Susie rose from her chair with Terry's aid. "Christoff. You can't kill Evangeline. She's human."

There was truth in Susie's statement, but she was only half right. Evangeline's blood was tainted with demon venom. Herein lay the problem. Damned either way, he would be obliged to kill her, but in doing so, he would be signing his own death warrant. Oddly, he didn't mind. True death would be a blessing. Living without her would be much worse. Considering her reaction to his last comment, he chose to keep this revelation to himself.

"Uhmm." Terry ran a finger around the inside of his collar as he grimaced. "That poses another problem. As much as I applaud the way you took out that degenerate in the pub, the law tends to come down hard on killers. Even if you manage to annihilate those ghouls, you'll be arrested and thrown into prison."

The color drained from Evangeline's face. Christoff guessed what she must be thinking. She'd lived alone for most of her life. A lone wolf. Free to roam whenever and wherever she wanted. Prison would kill not only her spirit, but her physical body. She'd not survive a month.

She grabbed his upper arms. Her fingernails dug into his skin as she leaned closer, tears brimming her lower lashes. "Promise me," she whispered. "I'm begging you." She closed her eyes. "If it comes to that, I want you to kill me. Don't let them lock me away."

****

Evangeline sat on the sand, her toes wiggling in the salt water as she tried to enjoy what she suspected would be her last day alive. The Corel family's private beach offered privacy. An invitation too good to pass up. She stripped down to her underwear and lay back in the sand, her semi-naked skin soaking up the last rays of sunlight as her thoughts drifted up to the cottage and the vampire who slept inside.

He'd keep his promise, of that she was sure. Honest to the point of rudeness, he would not have given his word if he'd not meant it. Everything else about the man, remained a mystery. Despite their heated argument, he'd still reached for her during the night. His large hands had cupped her breasts and squeezed until she'd pushed him away. When he rolled over, turning his back to her, she felt every cell in her body scream out in protest. If only she'd been able to control her temper one last time. She'd go to her grave regretting the lost opportunity to feel the strength in those large arms as they wrapped around her. Even now, her body responded to the images of their lovemaking. Her right hand slipped down between her legs to stroke her swollen clit.

"Yes, yes. It pleases me to see you fondle yourself."

She sat bolt upright. Her eyes hardly believing what she saw.

"Who the hell are you?" *This can't be happening. Please, please don't be him. Not now.* Crossing one arm over her chest, the other in front of her crotch, she tried to cover, not only the sheerness of her underwear, but also, her fear.

"Come, my daughter. Let *me* satisfy your carnal urges." He motioned to the bulge in his tight leather trousers as he thrust his hips forward. "And you, my dear, can appease mine."

The taste of bile soured her taste buds. An ugly, horned demon would have been easier to dismiss. Fear would have made her forget her embarrassment and revulsion. Unfortunately, this predator looked like he'd stepped from a fashion magazine. The color of his dark hair matched her own and his features and physique were aesthetically pleasing … for a fiend. Other than the unusual shade of purple in his irises, he could easily pass as human. She shook her head as she backed away to reach her discarded clothes. Another man who thought her body was his own private play toy.

"I think I'll pass. I'm not into incest."

The trek up to the cottage involved climbing at least twenty stairs. She'd be forced to turn her back on him. If he grabbed her from behind, she'd be helpless.

"Incest?" His laugh sent a chill down her spine. "Despite what you think, I am not your father."

"But… I thought –"

"The mystical arts are complicated, my dear." He maneuvered himself between Evangeline and the stairs. "Let me think how I can explain this." He scratched his chin and grinned. "My blood runs in your veins, but my sperm did not create you. I infected your DNA rather than contributed to it. It's rather like your vampire. His demon lives in his blood, however, it lives apart from him. They are two separate entities." He moved towards her. "So, shall we fornicate now?"

"Go fuck yourself." Her quaking voice didn't

sound as forceful as she'd hoped. She couldn't even convince her own legs that she was brave. They shook so violently, she could barely stand, let alone run.

His smile did little to bolster her confidence. "So, you want foreplay? I'm happy to oblige. It will make me even hornier. Go on, run. I'll even give you a head's start. I remember the children's game of hide and seek. Tell you what I'll do. I'll count to fifty and—"

She took off running, bolting past him and up the stairs, two at a time. There was no way she'd reach the cottage in the time it took him to count to fifty, but at least she could put some distance between them. She had to. Somehow, despite her revulsion, she was inexplicably drawn to him. It was as if she had no choice but to submit to his advances. Her own demon blood responded to him. So far, his words had been crude suggestions, he hadn't ordered her to obey him. Would she be able to fight his commandments?

Half way between the beach and the cottage, he caught her. She slammed into his body when he suddenly materialized in front of her. To her horror, her breasts felt the damp heat of his bare chest and she realised that he'd discarded his own clothes. His naked arousal pressed against her belly. His arms wrapped around her body. His lips claimed her, and his laughter reverberated into her mouth. "I think we have an audience."

She broke contact with his lips, turning her head towards the cottage and the man who stood by the window. Although a distance away, she could see the look of betrayal etched on his face. The pain in Christoff's eyes. As she struggled in the demon's arms, he whispered into her ear.

"You and I are simpatico. I believe you understand that, should I command it, you will give yourself to me. Shall we, to use your vernacular, fuck here in front of your friend, or go somewhere more private?"

She closed her eyes, but the image of Christoff's shattered expression remained permanently etched on her mind. *I may be part demon, but I'm not a monster. I won't force him to watch, even if it means I'm throwing away my only chance of escape.* She took a deep breath, knowing that her world was about to change, and not for the better. "Take us somewhere private."

****

Christoff drew the curtains and flopped down on the edge of the bed. He couldn't watch any more. He'd given her every chance to prove herself to be a decent human being and this is how she'd repaid him? The musk of her arousal had reached his finely tuned senses. Driven him from his bed in the hopes that she'd forgiven him for his insensitive remarks and waited for him to come to her. What a fool he'd been. He balled his hands into fists and fumed. *Whore.* Worse than that. A prostitute would have met her John in a private place. A seedy motel room where they could fornicate without the rest of the world being privy to their escapades. This woman had the gall to parade almost naked, outside his bedroom with another man. Judging by their body language, they were about to do the deed then and there.

Not while there's breath in my body.

He jumped to his feet and stormed out of the bedroom, through the living room and out the front door. Human or no, this man was going to die.

Outside the cottage, he stopped. Where were they? Surely, they hadn't time to leave the estate? Being an ancient, the last rays of sunlight did little more than prickle his skin. Soon it would be dark and even the tingling would stop. He strode down towards the beach, his hands fisting and releasing as he made his way to the secluded alcove, expecting the worst, planning his revenge. Besides a small hermit crab that quickly darted out of his way, the beach was empty. Out of the corner of his eye, he noticed a small heap of clothes. Evangeline's clothes. Looking around, he failed to find any others. Had the male come to the beach naked? He raised his arm, planning to throw the clothes far out into the water. That would teach her for making a fool of him. Something made him pause. He sniffed the air. Rotten eggs? Although faint, the smell of sulfur hung in the breeze. Holding the clothes close to his face, he inhaled. Evangeline's intoxicating scent clung to the fabric. He detected no trace of sulfur.

How was that possible? If a demon had seduced Evangeline, he would be able to detect at least a whiff of him on her belongings. Turning back to the stairs, Christoff noticed a beach towel draped over the rail. Had she come down to the beach for a dip and encountered the demon? Besides his own footprints, he noticed two other sets in the sand, plus, the larger imprint of a body. Drawing on his profiler techniques, he deduced two important things. Evangeline had been laying alone on the ground when the male approached wearing shoes. It was hardly likely that he wore shoes and nothing else, so, he must have been fully dressed when he advanced on her.

Beside the larger imprint, near where he found her clothes, the sand had been disturbed into a heap. A deep impression convinced him that she had dug her feet into the ground to push off running. He followed the stairs back up to the perfectly manicured lawn. Perfect, except for the divots where her feet had landed heavily. These were not produced by someone taking a leisurely stroll. She was running. Running for her life. He searched the area for more footprints and found none. Why would he?

The demon would not bother to chase his prey when he could easily materialize whenever he wanted.

"How could I be so foolish?"

He'd let long forgotten human emotions control his judgement. Christoff's heart slammed into his chest. What he'd witnessed wasn't Evangeline seducing a man. She was being assaulted by a demon.

****

They materialized in a darkened room, surrounded by cloaked and hooded figures. The heady aroma of incense hung in the air. Dazed from the teleportation, it took Evangeline a few moments to comprehend her situation and attempt to cover her body with her hands.

"I thought you were taking us somewhere private?"

His laugh curdled the contents of her stomach. His words, more so.

"My minions will not disturb us, my dear." He winked an eye before adding, "*Until* I give them the signal to participate."

"You sick, twisted bastard."

She pushed away from his embrace and scanned the room until she saw what she needed. With a flick of her wrist, she used her powers to snatch a robe from its wall hook and send it sailing to her outstretched hand. Once covered in the newly acquired garment, she found the confidence to challenge her abductor even further.

"If you or any of your goons try to touch me, I'll set fire to your gonads."

"I'd like to see you try that." He motioned to one of his followers. "Prepare her for the ritual."

The male rose, bowed and came at her with a carnal look in his eye.

She extended her arm, palm out, and threw him

against a wall. The sickening sound of cracking bone told her that she'd crossed the line long before he fell to the floor in a pool of blood. Before she had time to contemplate her actions, a wave of worshippers charged her. This time, flames shot from her hands, incinerating each in turn until only the demon remained.

The steady sound of his clapping chilled her to the bone. She doubted that Christoff and Terry would be as amused. She wondered which would be the least painful, lethal injection or fatal vampire bite?

"Impressive, I must say. I can only imagine how powerful you will be, once properly trained. Come, let us finish what we started at the beach."

"Finish *this*." Concentrating all her power into her palms, she sent a bolt of electricity through his body, lighting him up with blue sparks. His body convulsed, but remained upright as she continued to hit him with wave after wave of electrical energy. When his eyes rolled back into his head, she stopped, exhausted and confident she'd finished the job. She was wrong.

"Ah. I needed that." He squared his shoulders and grinned. "Thank you for the little-pick- me up. You look surprised. Did you really think you could kill me?" With a chuckle and a wave of his hand, his clothes materialized. "You are only a halfling. Only a demon can kill another." He glanced around the room at the piles of ash and broken bodies. "Such a mess. Fortunately, I have many other minions to take their place."

Many? She'd already killed at least ten people. How many others would die at her hands? She slumped against the brick wall and fought to catch her breath. Monster. *I've become my father.*

"Your reluctance has become tiresome." His statement shocked her back to reality. "If you aren't prepared to service me..." He raised an eyebrow. She shook her head. "Then return to the vampire until I call for you."

****

Christoff turned towards the gasp and did a double-take. A hooded figure lay sprawled on the sand covered in only a black cloak. The bare legs of a woman gave him hope.

"Evangeline?"

The woman lifted her head and removed the cowl from her face. Her eyes glistened with tears as he lifted her to her feet. "Oh, Chris. I didn't think I'd ever see you again."

Sending a silent prayer of thanks out to the universe, he hugged her close to his body and planted kisses on the top of her head. "And I, you, my precious. Where have you been?"

"I have no idea." Her tears dampened the silk of his shirt. "But there's something else I need to tell you."

"Do not fear my wrath." He lifted her chin with his finger. "I admit that seeing you with another man sent me into a rage, but I know now that he manipulated the situation. I know that you were not intentionally unfaithful to me. The demon failed in his attempt to turn me against you."

"I wasn't even unintentionally unfaithful." She corrected. "He stripped off his clothes as he caught me running away. What you saw was him catching me. Nothing happened."

She pulled the edges of the cloak together as her body shivered in the cold night air.

"You're cold?"

As she nodded her head, he scooped her into his arms and teleported into the cottage.

"I didn't know you could do that."

"There are many things you still don't know about

me." Some, he hoped she would never learn. Others, he longed to teach her. Sensual things. For the moment, he'd have to be patient. "I'll run a hot bath for you."

"We need to talk." She called to him from the bedroom. "There's something you should know."

A ball coiled in his belly. Part of him didn't want to know. The other, needed to know. Had she lied about fornicating with the demon? He strolled back into the room, trying to keep his emotions in check. "Did the demon seduce you? Wait. Did he –"

Her quick and violent reaction was all he needed to hear. "No. I wouldn't let him touch me."

"Then enjoy your bath and we will discuss the matter later."

He kissed her forehead and left the room. She'd be hungry and exhausted from her abduction. If he'd learned anything about Evangeline, it was her insatiable appetite. A pizza and bottle of merlot would lift her spirits. Whatever she had to tell him could wait.

****

Entering the bathroom felt like stepping into a romantic novel. The deep, freestanding tub needed a step to climb into. Scented candles bathed the room in a soft, warm light and cast beautiful reflections on the mirrored backsplash behind the tub. However, even the hot water and luxurious, thick bubbles of fragrant perfume could not relax the knots in her shoulders. The demon's blood bubbled inside her veins. Scorched her skin. Played tricks with her mind. He spoke to her constantly … or was it her own voice urging her to do unspeakable things?

Crockery rattled in the kitchen. The aroma of stone fired pizza drifted into the bathroom making her mouth water and her tummy rumble, but she had an appetite for something else. Sex, and lots of it.

"Come and get it."

His double-entendre sent a shiver down her spine and a rush of blood to her erogenous zones. As she stepped out of the bath, she questioned her heightened desires. After all the demon had said. After everything she'd been through. Surely sex would be the last thing she craved? Despite her doubts, she couldn't deny her body's almost painful arousal. When he suddenly appeared at the bathroom door, she gave in to her desires.

"Are you ready for dinner?" His eyes widened as his gaze drifted over her naked body. He let out a deep breath as she moved closer.

"I'm ready for something." He wanted her. She could see his arousal throbbing against the zipper of his trousers. Why then, did he reach out to hold her at arms' length? "Don't you want to make love to me?"

"Always." He murmured as she traced her fingers across his jawline. "Always and forever."

"Then take me. Here. Now."

He closed his eyes for a moment then re-opened them. "Are you sure you want to do this? You've been through an ordeal and may still be in shock. I'd be less of a man if I took advantage."

A ball of anger coiled in her belly. Heat scorched her skin. Did he want her or not? She offered him pleasure. Would he prefer pain? One way or another, she would quench her thirst. If he knows what's good for him, he'd better decide quickly.

"If you don't want me, don't make excuses." She turned her back to him and watched his reaction in the mirrored backsplash.

He looked confused, tormented, conflicted. One last push and he'd comply.

"If you really cared for me, you'd show me." She hid her grin inside. "I need you."

Wrapping his arms around her, he whispered into

her ear. "Tell me what you want. Let me prove my love."

Snap.

"Take off your clothes."

To her surprise, he removed them with a wave of his hand.

"Interesting." *Is that something I could learn to do?* "What else can you do?"

His fingers traced her skin, from her shoulders down to her hands. As he wove his fingers through hers, he smiled. "What would you like me to do?"

"Lots of naughty, wicked things."

When he tugged on her hand, drawing her to the bedroom, she shook her head. "If we're going to do dirty things, we should start in the bathroom."

He raised an eyebrow. "You want me to join you in the tub?"

"Not *yet.*" She bit her bottom lip and turned to face the mirrored wall.

"Perhaps you should instruct me. Tell me what you want me to do."

She smiled up at his reflection. His dilated pupils told her everything she wanted to know. Let the games begin.

"I love this tub, Christoff. The perfect height for a bath." She bent at the waist, pressing her sex against his throbbing erection. "Don't you just love sinking in deep? Feeling the rush of heat on your skin. Wrapped in a cocoon of damp, hot, pleasure."

"Yes." He groaned, as he entered her with a thrust of his hips. "Deep is very good."

Supporting her weight with her elbows, she leaned on the edge of the bath. "Do you know what else is nice?"

The rhythm of his thrusts sped up as he succumbed to her game. His heart pounded against her back while his lips caressed her neck. "Tell me, min dyrebare, tell me."

"The weight of my boobs in your palms. Your fingers squeezing and pinching my nipples into hard peaks."

He followed her instructions to the letter, but it was not enough. She wanted more. Needed more.

"Harder." She wailed, as the pressure increased. "I need to feel every inch of you driving into me."

His hips slammed against her buttocks with ever increasing speed. Their skin slapped together as if applauding their actions. Drops of perspiration fell from his forehead, hitting her back with a sizzle. So hot. When he released her breasts, digging his fingers into her hips, holding her tight as he drove into her, she raised her head and stared into the mirrored back-splash.

Hooded, purple eyes stared back at her from a flushed face. Dark, damp curls stuck to her cheeks and plump lips parted with a groan. With each thrust of their hips, her breasts swung like beautiful, over-ripe fruit, dripping from a sprinkling of summer rain. She'd seen her reflection many times, but never had she appreciated the perfection of a female body. The soft curves. The smooth skin. The sensual allure. Cupping her breasts, she delighted in the sensation of her own hands fondling the heavy orbs. More. Need more.

The reflection looked on as her right hand dropped between her legs and stroked her swollen clit. It smiled its appreciation as she pleasured both herself and Christoff simultaneously. They came together in a rush of adrenaline and heat that shook the room. Literally.

"It must be an earthquake." Christoff suggested as he dragged her down with him, using the doorframe for protection.

Evangeline knew better. Curled up on his lap, she

watched, mesmerized, as the mirror expanded and contracted, finally exploding. Shards of glass flew in all directions but the sting from the slivers of broken mirror did not compare to the pounding pain in her head. Zigzag lines blurred her vision and the familiar aura of flashing colors warned her of an impending migraine. She held her palms to her temples as the blinding pain became too much to bear. The ground beneath them shook. Floor tiles cracked as the concrete beneath it shifted. Strong arms curled around her, holding her, protecting her as the foundations of the house twisted and groaned. Would he hold her so affectionately if he knew that, somehow, she was causing the quakes? If this was the apocalypse that Christoff had mentioned? Would she be responsible for ending the world?

Chapter Eight

Christoff leaned back against the grandiose living room wall, crossed his arms over his chest and fumed. "I still think this is a bad idea."

"What choice do we have." His host, David reminded him. "The cottage is in dire need of repair. It isn't safe."

"I have to agree with Christoff," the pretty blonde woman reminded her husband. "Tell him what you told me, Anna."

Aware that his presence caused unease, Christoff uncrossed his arms and found a vacant chair beside Susie. Her warm smile reminded him that he had at least one ally in the group. As for the other five … only time would tell. David and his wife, Meaghan, were at odds. He wanted to keep Evangeline close at all times, so they could monitor her movements, while his wife was reluctant. As for David's brother, Derrick, he sided with his own wife, Anna, who warned them of disaster. The family's resident witch was none too happy about having someone as powerful as Evangeline in their home.

"Look, Christoff, surely you can understand our concerns. The last time we dealt with a demon, we nearly lost Meaghan and Terry." Pointing to Susie, she added. "What if that thing attacks Susie and her baby?"

"That *thing* has a name. I'd thank you to remember that." He leaned forward in his chair as the blood bubbled in his veins. "Do you really believe that I would risk her or the baby? I'd give my life for them."

Susie placed her hand on his as she whispered. "Calm down, big guy. No one doubts your loyalty."

Anna frowned. "You know very well I was referring to the demon, not the woman, Christoff. I feel for her. Truly I do. But I sense an evil presence in the house."

Christoff jumped to his feet. "She. Is. Not. Evil." As he leaned towards her, Derrick stepped between them.

"Must I remind you that you are a guest in this house." He turned to his brother for support. "Is this really what you want?"

"Brothers." David pushed the posturing men apart. "Let's discuss this like civilized people."

"He is not my brother." Christoff growled under his breath. "I have no brothers."

"You're wrong." His host maneuvered him back to his seat. "Everyone here shares a connection. We are family. Joined by a blood bond that cannot be broken."

There was a truth to David's words that Christoff could not deny. They did, indeed, share a bond much stronger than a regular family. The blood that ran in their veins carried with it the original host. Much like Evangeline, they each carried at least part of the demon, only their intruder required little more from them than a regular supply of blood.

"Would it be easier if she came to stay with us for a while?" Susie offered.

The room resounded with an emphatic no. At least they all agreed on something.

"Maybe I could have her thrown in lock-up. Those walls are pretty damned thick."

Christoff answered Terry's suggestion with a snarl. Evangeline would rather die than be locked away. None of the comments or ideas took Evangeline's feelings into account. They didn't understand her. Another reason why he always worked alone.

"I made a mistake bringing her here. I should have handled it on my own. When she wakes, I'll take her far away where she won't be able to do any harm."

"Look, Lurch, don't get your knickers in a knot. We're all on your side." Terry sat on the arm of Susie's chair and took her hand in his. "Even *you* should understand our apprehension after seeing how she mangled half the town."

Christoff leaned to the side and glanced towards the entrance to the living room. "She thinks I believe it was an earthquake. Until we know exactly what happened, I prefer she continues to think that."

"Fine with me. After what she did to that guy in the bar, I wouldn't want to do anything to upset her." Terry's eyebrows drew together. "That reminds me. With the APB out on her, she can't really leave the house anyway. I'm sticking my neck out covering for her." He turned to David. "We all are."

Meaghan turned to her husband. "Guy in the bar? What's he talking about?"

David shrugged. "First I've heard of it."

"Great detectives you two are." Terry shook his head and sighed. "Lucky you have me to help run the place."

Susie slapped his hand. "And me." She addressed Meaghan's question. "Some creep attacked Evangeline in a bar. He and his thugs planned to assault her in the alley behind the building. She sent one to the hospital and the others packing."

Christoff watched David's expression turn from interest to concern. His shoulders squared, and his voice took on the authoritarian tone of the coven's leader.

"She attacked a human? Why was I not informed?"

"She *is* a human." Susie reminded him. "And it was self-defense."

"Only half-human." Anna interjected. "And growing less human every day."

"Enough." Christoff bellowed. "I will not stand here and listen to any more of your insults. Evangeline and I will leave this house immediately. If any of you try to stop me—"

"Stand down." David ordered him. "In light of this revelation, I must insist that she stays where we can watch her." He turned to the couple sitting in the corner. "While she is living here, you must not visit. I need your promise on that."

"You have mine." Terry told him.

"Fine." Susie pouted. "But you can't stop me contacting her by phone."

Fighting the unusual compulsion to hug his little friend, Christoff chose to instead show his appreciation with a smile. She returned it with one of her own. Despite being the most fragile of the group, Susie had the biggest heart and balls to match. Evangeline could benefit from a friend like her.

"She will awaken soon. I must see to her needs."

He marched from the room without uttering another word to the group. Deep down, he knew their reservations were well founded. He'd seen the purple eyes reflected in the mirror, minutes before the room began to shake. But he could also sense Evangeline's conflict. He'd lived with his own demon long enough to recognize another. If only he could think of a way to stop the demon without hurting Evangeline.

"Wait."

He turned to the direction of the voice. David strolled over and placed a hand on his shoulder.

"You mustn't judge us on words spoken out of fear, old friend. We have come to learn that the demon's followers are involved in child sacrifice. Susie isn't like us, she's—"

"She's stronger than any of us and more important

to me than you realize. No harm will come to her or the child while there is breath in my body."

David let out a sigh as he leaned against the doorframe. "There is another matter to discuss. At the risk of incurring your wrath, I must remind you of your duties. If your gypsy woman kills an innocent human—"

"I know my duty." Christoff growled to his superior as he marched away. "If or when the time comes, I will do what needs to be done."

****

Evangeline stretched and opened her eyes to unfamiliar surroundings. As she opened her mouth to call for Christoff, he opened the door and entered the room.

"Where am I?"

"Our hosts have moved us to the main house on the estate while renovations are done to restore the cottage."

Although beautifully decorated, the room did not suit her at all. Too pretty with its pink curtains and matching bedcover. Everything in the room looked too dainty for a woman as rough and clumsy as herself. *No. I'm not staying here. No way, Jose.*

"Why can't we stay in my van? It won't take much to fix the door and cupboards. I should have done it earlier, but we were—"

He came to her side. His expression as serious as the day he told her about her mother's death. *Oh, great. What now?*

"Your mobile home was completely destroyed when … the earthquake hit. The spare fuel canister exploded and took out half the cottage with it."

Stomach churning, she gazed up at the ceiling and hoped beyond hope. "Please tell me you at least saved my clothes."

His answer was written on his face.

"Shit." She fell back onto the bed and slammed her fists down on the mattress. "Shit, shit, shit."

"We'll buy you new clothes."

"I don't want new clothes, I want *my* clothes." Even to her own ears, she sounded like a brat. What he said next made her feel even worse.

"We can't always have what we want."

Part of her wanted to correct him. Tell him that, in her case, we can't *ever* have what we want. Was it too much to dream of a happy, stable home life? Too greedy to want a man to love her for herself and not the person he expected her to be?

"I'm sorry. That was rude of me." He leaned over her and stroked her face. "I've been told that I don't have filters. Also, it seems I don't mix well with others."

"Really?" The corner of her mouth curled. "I never would have guessed."

"Your sarcasm isn't lost on me." He snickered as he rose from the bed. "Give me a few minutes, I'll ask the ladies of the house if they could lone you some clothes until we can go shopping."

"What? You don't like what I'm wearing?" She scooted from under the sheets and twirled for his approval.

"I like *my* bathrobe very much."

Funny, she didn't remember putting his bathrobe on. Her last memory was sitting naked in Christoff's lap as the world shook around her. He must have wrapped her in his robe to carry her to the main house. His chivalry deserved a reward. Dropping the garment from her shoulders, she let it fall to the floor.

"How about now? Do you like my birthday suit?"

His eyes widened in appreciation, but his eyebrows drew together. "I don't understand. You would go naked to a birthday celebration?"

Rolling her eyes, she sighed. *Forgot who I was talking to.* "You are such a dick sometimes. This is the suit I was born in. Get it? Birthday suit."

He curled his arms around her waist and drew her in for a kiss that literally took her breath away. Her body instantly responded to him. Barely had his tongue entered her mouth and she could feel her orgasm building. She dragged him down onto the bed and wrapped her legs around his waist.

"Hurry, Christoff."

"I'll be back soon, I promise." He whispered against her cheek. "The others are just outside. Do you really want them to hear us? I will return with the clothes and," he lifted up from her to wink, "I'll show you *my* birthday suit."

"No. Can't wait. Too close."

She could feel the pressure building between her legs as her womb clenched. Arching her back, she grabbed his hand and placed it at the source of her discomfort.

"Give a girl a hand, will you?" She curled her hands around his head and pulled him down. His lips claimed hers. His tongue danced inside her mouth and his fingers worked their magic on her clit. The pressure of his hand … perfect. The steady clockwise motion … flawless. Her orgasm … thunderous.

"Don't stop." She screamed into his mouth as her body convulsed against his palm. "Oh, Chris. Oh, fuck, yes."

The voice in her head rejoiced. *Yes. I believe living inside your curvaceous body will have many advantages. The female orgasm is a new, and very pleasant experience. Shall we go again?*

"Get off me." Evangeline pushed against Christoff with her palms.

"But I thought –"

"Just go." She snatched the robe off the floor and, turning her back, put in on.

"Did I do something wrong?" His hands gently brushed her shoulders.

The confusion in his voice broke her heart. Although her body craved his touch, she couldn't give in to the desires, knowing that they were not her own. The demon's lust was becoming insatiable. He had plans for her body once he took it over completely. Plans that did not sit well with her. His quest for physical pleasure almost exceeded his desire for causing pain. With her self-control slipping, she couldn't risk being around Christoff.

"You promised me some clothes." She reminded him, without turning around. How could she face him without giving in to the urges? The urge to screw him. To hurt him. To kill him.

His hands left her shoulders. The silence in the room became almost deafening until, finally, relief came with the clicking of the door.

****

Christoff was still scratching his head as he made his way back to the living room. What had he done to upset her? Hadn't he satisfied her needs adequately? Her groans sounded like those of appreciation for his technique. Why had she suddenly dismissed him?

As he entered the room, the reaction of the occupants varied.

Susie blushed a bright shade of pink while the other women avoided his eye contact. The brothers Corel smirked, but Palmer broadly smiled as he sauntered over to slap Christoff's back.

"Sounds like you 'saw to her needs' thoroughly, Lurch. Funny. I never pegged you for a five-minute wonder. Always thought you'd have staying power."

"What the hell are you talking about, Palmer?" He brushed the man's hand away and glared.

"Your sexual prowess." Terry grinned widely. "By the way, have you ever heard the expression, "payback's a bitch"? How does it feel having your private moments shared with others?"

Christoff glanced around the room. "Could someone tell me what this man's talking about?"

David filled a glass with the liquid from a blood bag and handed it to him. "To use your vernacular, he's referring to the sounds of you and Evangeline, fornicating your brains out only meters away from us." He motioned to Terry and Susie. "Even those without super-human hearing could tell what was happening."

So what? His woman had needs and he satisfied them. Surely that only proved him to be a competent and generous lover? Besides, they were wrong in their assumptions.

"We did not fornicate." He told them as he finished his drink in one gulp and handed back the glass for a refill. "I merely—"

"Saw to her needs." Terry chuckled. "Yeah, you told us you were going to do that. I didn't know you meant literally."

Anna helped Susie to her feet as vampire and detective squared up.

"Ladies, I think it's time we left the men to their own devices."

"Wait." Christoff pushed Terry aside as he addressed the women. "Evangeline lost everything in the fire. Could I impose on you to loan her something until I have the opportunity to take her shopping?"

"Of course." Meaghan nodded. "I'll rustle up something straight away." In seconds, she'd disappeared up the stairs and returned with an armful of clothes. "I'm not sure if these will fit well. Her body shape is more voluptuous than mine and, from what I've been told, she's tall."

He took the clothes and nodded his thanks. Yes. His woman had the stature of an amazon and her body curved in all the right places. The very thought of her stirred his blood. If only he could understand her and what was going on in that beautiful mind of hers.

"I think she'll need this, too." David handed him a box containing a brand new iPhone. "I understand her phone was stolen. This one is set up for her with her old number. I've taken the liberty of having a tracking device added. That way, we will know where she is at all times."

Christoff opened his mouth to protest, but closed it without saying a word. David was right. They needed to keep track of her comings and goings. Considering her recent volatile mood swings, her struggle with the demon must be escalating. As strong as she was, he worried for both her sanity and her soul.

"As much as I'd like to stay and hear more about big guy's sex life," Terry interrupted as he hooked his arm around Susie. "The sun is almost up, and I need to get this one home, so I can start work."

"I've fortified the perimeter of your house." Anna kissed her friend goodbye. "Nothing is going to be able to get in."

Christoff resisted the urge to argue Evangeline's innocence. The mystical protection was probably a good idea considering the recent events. Susie's humanity left her vulnerable and her pregnancy even more fragile to supernatural attack. As much as he loved and trusted Evangeline, he knew the power of the demon.

When Susie rose on tip toe to kiss his cheek, she whispered in his ear. "She can beat this, Christoff. With

AND NOW YOU'RE MINE

you at her side, she'll defeat him."

He smiled his thanks, then turned to Terry. "Keep me informed about any other supernatural events."

"Yes, sir."

Even Christoff recognized his salute as sarcastic.

"We all want to be kept in the loop," David reminded Palmer. "Things can escalate pretty quickly. I don't want any more nasty surprises."

Nasty surprises? Was he referring to Evangeline? Before he could comment, he noticed the subtle shaking of Susie's head and the knocking at his cerebral door.

They mean well. She told him. *You're upset and taking offense too easily. Go to her. She must be feeling very insecure.*

With a nod, he left the room, but Susie's voice followed him. *I'm here if you need me.*

****

"Who did you borrow these clothes from? A pint-sized Pollyanna?"

Evangeline gazed at her reflection in the floor length mirror. The short floral dress barely covered her bottom and her breasts threatened to pop out from the neck. Although made from a stretchable material, the garment clung to her body like a second skin. She reached down and held up the daisy sandals with her index finger.

"You're shitting me. Daisies? Who in the hell wears daisy sandals? Is David's wife twelve?"

"Meaghan meant well." Christoff told her with an expression that reminded her that her words had been ungrateful. She hadn't even met the Corel family and they'd opened up their home to her.

"Look, Chris. I appreciate the clothes, really, I do. It's just that—"

"They don't suit your personality."

"Not to mention, they don't fit." She leaned forward and placed the shoe beside her foot. "At least two sizes too small for my huge feet." Motioning to her breasts, she added, "And look at these puppies about to escape the kennel."

"I can't take my eyes off them." His eyebrows lifted, and a smile spread from cheek to cheek. "Also, your feet are perfect. Everything about you is perfect."

His features softened as he moved towards her with outstretched arms. She rushed into them and snuggled into the warmth of his embrace, drawing strength from his adoration. Could he really see perfection where she only saw flaws? Was his love enough to drive the demon away? If she told him the truth, would he, could he understand?

"I need to ask you something."

"What is it, min dyrebare?"

She led him over to a settee beside the block out curtains covering the bay window. The bed posed too many temptations. Besides, her questions were more important than her sexual needs.

"Tell me about my father?"

His hesitation gave her cause for concern. Was her father really so evil?

"Your paternal line consisted of many mages, but until your father, most dealt with white magic. My sources told me that, once he'd tasted the power of black magic, he became obsessed with the need to learn more about the forces of darkness. Drunk on mystical energy, he summoned the demon to do his bidding, but demons are notorious tricksters. It convinced him to give himself completely over, even change his name to that of the demon."

"I knew that my mother kept her maiden name and registered my name Russo. Are you saying that my father *changed* his name to Lupescu?"

"Not just his Surname. Mánagarmr is the demon's Christian name. It means 'devourer'.""

Almost afraid to ask, she steadied herself for her next question. "And Lupescu? What does that mean?"

"Moon wolf."

Palms together, she held her fingertips against her mouth. "I'm guessing that means something?"

With a nod he answered. "The medallion symbolizes a wolf swallowing the moon. We assume that the demon identifies with the Fenris wolf from the Norse Ragnarok legend."

Not just the moon, my dear. The entire world. With our combined power and my knowledge, we will destroy this world and create a better one.

A shiver ran down her spine. Was that even possible?

"Are you all right?"

"No." She stared up into his glacial blue eyes. "No, Chris. I'm not all right. Far from it."

"What can I do to help you?"

"You can kill me."

He recoiled at her request. His brows knit, and his lips tightened into a straight line.

"I couldn't even if I wanted to. Trust me. Nothing could convince me to kill you."

As she sprung to her feet, she challenged him. "What if I told you I'd taken a human life?"

"I don't believe you." He glared his disbelief as he rose to face her. "Why would you say such a thing?"

Shoulders squared, she blurted out the entire story then corrected her previous statement. "Not just one human, ten. I deserve to die. You said so yourself."

Grabbing her by the shoulders, he argued. "When I said those things, I did not know you. The real you. If you killed those people, it was surely self-defense."

Did he know her? Maybe the other Evangeline, the real Evangeline might have killed in self-defense, but soon that woman would be gone. Every minute brought her closer to the edge of darkness. She balanced on a precipice, waiting for the inevitable plunge into the abyss. The demon's control clouded her mind, waiting for the right moment to take over. Even now, she could hardly tell what thoughts were her own and what belonged to him. All she knew for sure was that it was only a matter of time before he took her over completely.

"Please, Chris. I don't want to hurt anyone else."

"And you won't. I believe in you."

Even as his arms drew her in for a kiss, the demon encouraged her.

The fool trusts you. It will be easy to lure him to his death. First, we must kill the others. I cannot come inside the house, so you must come out to me. Find me in the garden and I will give you a weapon suited to killing vampires. Hurry. I have waited many years for the pleasure of destroying the vampire who entombed me in the medallion.

As hard as she tried, she couldn't stop her legs from moving towards the door.

"I need some time outside by myself. Time to think."

He flopped back onto the bed and half-smiled. "I'll be here."

"I'm counting on that." She told him, before leaving the room.

We both are.

****

After closing the bedroom door, Evangeline turned and gasped. Had she been transported to a palace? The Italian tiles beneath her bare feet were immaculate.

The pristine white and gold pattern too clean for the likes of her. Despite her profession as a scammer taking her to the most affluent homes in town, this one took the cake when it came to luxury. On tip toe, she crept down the long corridor, past what looked like a living room and into the kitchen. Beyond that, she could see the handles of sliding doors poking from behind heavy, block out curtains.

As she reached to slide open the door, she paused. Can't let him force me to hurt anyone. Especially Chris. Her fingers tightening around the handle until they turned white. There must be another way.

I grow impatient. The demon told her.

"Fuck you." She answered aloud, but still, she slid open the door and stepped outside.

Holding her hand above her face to shield her eyes from the sun, she made her way down the balcony steps, through the beautifully maintained tropical garden and past the swimming pool. There, on the meticulously manicured lawn, he waited. Unlike their last encounter, he wore a black suit with matching shirt and tie and stood with his legs apart, hands firmly on his hips.

Arrogant prick.

"Here." He held out an ornate handled dagger. "The steel has been magically tempered. Contrary to popular opinion, wooden stakes are not as effective in the disposal of vampires."

Drawing on all her courage, she spat at his face. He wiped the spittle off his cheek with the back of his suit sleeve but kept his other arm, and the dagger, extended.

With a shake of her head, she gave him instructions of her own.

"You can stick that thing up your ass. I won't be listening to any more of your commands."

"Won't you?" the demon laughed. "We'll see about that."

Blinding pain stabbed at her temples, driving her to her knees. She glared up at him from her position on the ground. "Is that all you've got, asshat?"

"Not even close."

The scream caught in her throat as her uterus twisted. Invisible knives stabbed at her internal organs. Blood trickled down between her legs and she began to lose consciousness as he leaned over her and whispered.

"Don't force me to injure your reproductive organs. I have plans for your womb."

"I. Will. Never. Have sex. With you." She gasped as another contraction tore through her body, forcing her to curl into the fetal position on the lawn.

"Sex? No, my dear." He chuckled. "I've lost interest in that notion."

She raised her head and struggled to open her eyes. "I don't understand. How—"

Twirling the blade around between his fingers, he crouched down on his haunches, so his face was inches away from hers.

"I grow tired of the body I'm presently inhabiting. He was a poor substitute for your father, but a necessary evil, pardon the pun. When your vampire killed him, he took away my powers. I was forced to wait until your blood brought me back from the ether."

Straightening the cuff links of his silk shirt, he smirked. "I needed a temporary, but willing vessel. This one, although aesthetically pleasing, had no power of his own. You exceed your father in natural abilities and your beauty outshines my current physical form. As a matter of fact, the sensations I experienced while inside your mind, have convinced me that the female form offers more pleasures. More sins of the flesh. When I'm bored with the many lovers, I will create my own offspring and together we will rule the world."

"No." Evangeline forced herself to her knees then up to her feet, almost clipping the demon's chin as she threw her head up. "I will never let you take control of my body. I will fight you tooth and nail, every step of the way."

"I love your spirit." He chuckled as he threw the dagger down at her feet. "We'll make a formidable union, you and I. Now pick up the weapon and kill the vampire." His eyes shimmered as a smile spread across his face. "On second thought, kill *all* the vampires who reside in this house."

Backing away, she shook her head. "Never. I will never hurt anyone in that house."

"You didn't seem to have a problem killing my minions." His mouth curled at the side, sending a wave of nausea up her throat. "And you did it, rather spectacularly, I might add."

Her heart pounded against her chest and her breath became labored. Something in his eyes worried her. Her body reacted with a cold shiver that ran down her spine.

"They … were evil, like you."

"Were they? Or were they under my compulsion?" He moved closer with steady, casual steps until she could smell his cologne. "Did you ever stop to wonder? Would you have cared?"

The ground beneath her feet became unsteady, or was it the violent shaking in her legs? She hadn't stopped to consider if they were under a spell before she incinerated each and every one of them. Self-preservation had been her only thought. That, and escaping the demon. Had she really murdered a group of innocents? Would she do it again under similar circumstances?

"Face it, Evangeline. Your vampire has sworn to protect the innocent. It's either you or him now. One of you must die."

His arrogant expression sickened her. Had this been his plan all along?

"You smug bastard. You forced me to kill those people just to piss off Chris."

Slapping his thigh, he laughed. "Of course I did, my dear. That, and instigating your disagreement at the bar. Unfortunately, instead of witnessing you killing the thug, he managed to talk you out of it. Damn shame."

Tears burned behind her eyes as she shook her head. "All this, just to punish Chris for killing Dad?"

The laughter stopped abruptly. "You think this is about your vampire?"

"I…" If not Chris, who? "You ordered me to kill him. I thought—"

"Killing your lover is a test of your obedience. He is inconsequential."

Blood pounded in her head making his words even harder to understand. Wasn't this all about Chris? Hadn't he insinuated that the metal scroll inside the medallion had been a curse on him?

"You look confused." After a quick glance at his watch, he added, "we still have a few hours before the vampires are at full strength. Ask me. Ask me the question that has twisted your beautiful face into a mask of worry lines, then you'll understand why you have no choice but to obey me."

No choice? Surely there was always a choice? At the very least, she could stall his plans. Maybe drag out the questions until the household awoke.

"The medallion contained a curse tablet." With a deep breath, she straightened her shoulders and stared into his eyes. "What was written on the scroll?"

"Ah, at last. The two-million-dollar question." His smile sickened her to her stomach, but he appeared content to answer. Maybe even eager. "Your father was egotistical to the point of gullible. When he heard that the great Christoff Berg was hunting him, he tried to make another bargain with me. I promised that he would not die *if* he allowed me to enter his body. Of course, once inside, I obliterated all that was left of him."

"So, you lied to him." Why did that not surprise her?

"Haven't you heard? Demons are notorious tricksters. If he was half the mage he imagined himself to be, he would have known that only *I* would benefit from the pact."

What a stupid man her father must have been. Vain and power hungry. She hoped that he burned in hell for what he'd done to her and especially her mother. Chris did the right thing, killing him. But things still didn't add up. Arms crossed over her chest, she probed for more answers.

"You still haven't answered my question. If it wasn't a curse on Chris, what *was* on the scroll?"

With a wave of his hand, the locket appeared in his palm. He opened it, took out the scroll, carefully unrolled it with his fingertips and read it aloud.

"Let her life bring me glory. Let her blood give you life."

The strength left her legs. She dropped to the ground, beside the dagger, unable to move. Her life? Her blood? Had her father really planned to sacrifice her for power? The demon showed no concern for her despair. Why should he? He circled her, staring down as if confused by her reaction to the writing on the tablet.

"A binding contract. You belong to me."

"But…"

"You want to know why you weren't sacrificed? After I seized your father's body, I had no use for you. However, with news of Berg's impending arrival, I had to take precautions. I sealed the tablet inside the medallion and, after my untimely death, I waited in the ether for you to break the seal."

As she lifted her chin to face him, she knew that her fate had been sealed along with the tablet. "Why all the drama? The library, the restaurant? You sent those people after me. You played with my mind *and* my body. Why not just take me over and be done with it?"

He touched his finger to his nose. "Ah, that's the real problem." As he motioned with his palms, her body rose in the air and she landed on her feet. "You see, I can't simply take over a body, especially someone as powerful and ... shall we say, pig-headed as you."

A glimmer of hope raised her blood pressure, the adrenaline empowered her to act. "Then that's that. Piss off and leave me alone."

She raised both arms. Electricity crackled at her fingertips as she pointed to him. The demon's eyes widened, and his mouth opened to form an O shape, but his words didn't have time to escape before he sailed through the air and down the garden steps. She followed him, lifted him, and hurled him against the jagged rocks at the edge of the beach. Again, and again, he slammed into the sharp edges, his bones cracking, his blood weeping into large pools at his feet.

As he tried to shimmer away, she threw his battered body into the water, far out to sea. For a moment, only bubbles disturbed the calm water, then, an arm reached upward, followed by his head. He gasped for air. Terror widened his eyes. She looked in the direction of his gaze as a fin broke the surface and began to circle. When it disappeared under the water, she held her breath, wishing and hoping it would finish the job she'd started. With a mighty leap, the shark torpedoed up, engulfing the body, lifting him into the air, before plunging back into the deep.

She dropped to the sand as a torrent of red foam bubbled to the surface. It was over.

Chapter Nine

"One hundred dollars for a pair of jeans? You've got to be shitting me?"

The saleswoman gasped and looked to Christoff for, what he suspected was support. He tried to hide his amusement. Neither he, nor the woman had any chance of besting Evangeline in a battle of wits.

"The price is quite reasonable for the quality, Miss."

Evangeline turned to Christoff. "She's trying to rip you off, Chris. I could buy five pairs for the same price on the other side of town."

The woman opened her mouth to speak, but Christoff silenced her with an ice-cold stare. He'd spent a fortune in this store over the years. Is she wanted her commission, she'd better remember … the customer is always right. Forcing a smile, the saleswoman excused herself under the premise of finding more clothes for her belligerent customer to try on.

When she'd left, Evangeline continued her protest as she tugged at his sleeve.

"Seriously. Let's go."

"We'll go, *after* we've replaced all of your old clothes." He crossed his arms, hoping that she'd give up and accept her fate. They'd be leaving with new clothes.

"Fine." She leaned in close, her eyes wide, her chin jutting forward. "If that's the case, you'd better take me to Old Navy or Ross's. Better still, a Goodwill store. That's where I bought my old clothes."

"Humor me." He caught her chin between his finger and thumb and pulled her in for a short kiss. "I had to pull a few strings to have the store open late. At least try on some of the clothes."

Before she could answer, the saleswoman returned with an armful of clothes and disappeared into the changeroom.

Evangeline rolled her eyes and mouthed an expletive at him before joining her.

He sat back in the large, comfortable guest chair and contemplated his future. The last few days had been joyful and, thankfully, uneventful. Other than complaining about the fit of the borrowed clothing, Evangeline had seemed happy and untroubled. They'd made arrangements to collect her mother's remains from the funeral home and find a suitable place for her ashes. If the demon had contacted her, she'd kept the information to herself. Still, he worried. Why had the attacks on Evangeline suddenly ceased? What was it planning? When asked, she'd told him that she didn't expect to see the demon again, but she refused to elaborate. He'd watched for signs and saw none. Why then did he have a sinking feeling that the worst was yet to come?

****

"That saleswoman must rub her hands together in glee when you walk in her store."

Despite her annoyance, she couldn't help but feel excited about her new clothes. Finally, after three days of agony, she'd be able to wear something without little flowers or animal patterns. Meaghan had a heart of gold, but the fashion sense of a ten-year-old.

Evangeline could hardly wait to show Christoff what was under the denim skirt and tank top, although the price of the underwear irked her. Where did the store get off charging three hundred dollars for the flimsy scraps of lace and satin? Still, she'd make sure he got his money's worth with the sexy striptease she'd planned for later. Better still, she might even slip out of the panties at the restaurant and pass them to him during dinner as a hint of what to expect for dessert. Smiling to herself, she clung to his arm as they walked down the street to where they'd parked the car. He raised an eyebrow and smiled.

"Why do I have the impression that you're planning something?"

"You'll just have to wait and see—"

"Hey. If it isn't Lurch. What are you doing in this neck of the woods?"

She recognized them immediately. Terry Palmer and his soon to be wife, Susie.

"Looks like you've been shopping." Susie patted her belly as she spoke. "I'm going to have to do that soon. My clothes are getting a bit tight. Maybe you'd like to come with me, Evangeline? I don't think this one will be any help." She tilted her head towards Terry who looked slightly annoyed.

"Sure, I'd be happy to." She tried to ignore the exchange of looks between the two men as they reacted to Susie's invitation. Did they doubt her choice of clothes or was it more than that?

Susie's melodious voice interrupted her train of thought.

"We're heading out to dinner."

"Yeah, she's not only got her appetite back, it's doubled." Terry interrupted.

His remark earned him a scowl before Susie turned her attention back to Evangeline. "Would you like to join us?"

Damn. There goes the panties under the table idea. As she prepared to agree, another voice interrupted. One that she'd hoped was gone forever. One that raised every hair on her body and churned the contents of her stomach.

Miss me?

As the temperature of her skin rose and sweat began to bead on her forehead, Evangeline tried to remain calm. She'd fought him before and won. She could do it again. He'd admitted that he needed permission to take over her body and that sure as hell wasn't going to happen any time soon. Christoff frowned his confusion while Terry and Susie looked uncomfortable as they waited for her answer. What could she do?

"Sure. That'll be great."

****

As she slipped her hand into his, Christoff gave it a squeeze and led her after the others as they hurried to the restaurant. Apparently, Terry hadn't exaggerated about Susie's appetite because they almost had to run to keep up. The décor seemed a bit kitsch for his taste, but then again, he rarely ate out and never in a group. Somehow, he didn't mind the new experiences or the company.

After the waiter took their orders, he noticed the flush in Evangeline's cheeks and leaned in to whisper his concern.

"Are you unwell?"

"I'm fine."

Neither her forced smile, nor her words convinced him. What was she hiding? He closed his eyes and sighed. *Of course.* Her last experience in a restaurant had ended badly. It's only natural that she'd have reservations about dinner, especially with people she hardly knew. He slid his hand over her thigh and squeezed, hoping his smile might reassure her.

"So." Susie chirped, from her seat apposite Evangeline. "Can I pencil you in for a shopping trip next week?"

"Wouldn't Anna or Meaghan be a better choice?" She'd seen photos of the women in the living room of the mansion. Photos taken before they'd been turned. Both women were gorgeous and dressed like the covers of Vogue magazine.

"They've gone away for a romantic weekend with their hubbies. Besides, I don't feel comfortable in the stores where they shop. Please, please, please come with me?"

Evangeline shrugged. "I guess so, but are you sure you want me to help you choose?" she motioned to her ensemble. "I'm a bit rough around the edges."

"Rubbish." Susie scowled. "I love your fashion sense. Besides, I'm going to be the hippest, coolest mom in town with your help."

"Hip? Cool?" Terry choked on his drink of water. "Not using those outdated words, hun."

Christoff listened to the playful banter with amusement. Despite the back and forth of what seemed to him to be insults, he sensed the affection in both the tone and rhythm of the words. Moreover, he enjoyed the way the conversation brought a smile to Evangeline's lips. She, too, found amusement in the conversation and even joined in at times to defend Susie.

He leaned back in his seat, crossed his arms over his chest and drank in the joyfulness as his companions worked like a tonic to his broken soul. According to Evangeline, the demon was gone, which usually meant it was time to move on. Somehow, he could not contemplate leaving Azure Waters or his new friends. *Friends*? Is that what they were? He'd never stayed in one place long enough to know how it felt. Even David was more of a brother than a friend, until now. Now ... he had no compulsion to leave any of them, especially Evangeline.

Another roar of laughter drew his attention back to the conversation. Evangeline wiped away tears as she composed herself. At first, he assumed the obvious and smiled to think she'd grown comfortable with their companions. However, behind the joyful tears, he saw real sorrow and reached to touch her hand. She turned to him, rewarded him with a half-smile, then excused herself from the table.

"But our food's just arrived," Susie protested, as the waiter placed the meals on the table.

"I won't be long." Evangeline promised. She took one step away from the table, then turned back to Christoff. With a hand on each of his cheeks, she drew his face to hers and kissed him deeply. "I love you," she whispered, leaving before he could reciprocate.

****

Christoff's key in hand, she hurried back to the car while the demon reminded her how he would punish her if she changed her mind.

"Alright, you fucker, you've won. I'm on my way. At least give me some time to myself and my own thoughts until we've sealed the deal."

Beside the car, she froze. Would she be strong enough to pull this off? The deserted street only added to her pain. Alone again. She'd lived most of her life on the road, trying to make the money to save her mother. If only she'd tried honesty instead of trickery. Maybe if she'd asked Christoff for the money, her mother would be... No. Chris's doctors had said that there was nothing to be done. What could conventional medicine do to counteract demon blood? Anger bubbled up from her core. The demon might think he was going to win, but she had other plans.

****

"Hello, again."

Evangeline sized up the middle-aged man who waited for her on the private beach and recognized him as the guy from the library. His clothes still reeked of menthol and body odor.

"You've sunk to a new low," she told the demon. "Couldn't you have found someone less repulsive?"

The man shrugged. "This one accepted me without hesitation. You see, my dear, killing is in his nature." The corner of his mouth curled into a sneer and he winked. "If you do not comply, he will take great delight in slicing up your pretty friend and her fetus."

"If you touch her…"

"You'll what? Face it. If I want her dead, there's nothing you can do to stop it. She's human and vulnerable while her vampire friends are sequestered in their home during the day. All I have to do is—"

"Stop it." Evangeline took a deep breath. "I've agreed to your terms, now, give me what I asked."

The demon opened his hand and held his palm out flat to reveal two metal scrolls.

"You're a clever little gypsy. I can't wait to start our journey together."

She snatched the scrolls from his hand and carefully unrolled them one at a time. The first was the new contract, promising that he'd never hurt Susie, the baby, or anyone else in the group. The second made her sick to her stomach. How could her father give her away to a demon? With one final look, she spat on the offending object and threw it to the sand.

"Destroy it."

He smiled as blue flames shot from his fingertips, hitting the scroll with a force that left nothing but a haze of yellow dust in its wake. "Satisfied?"

She held out her hand, palm up.

"The locket."

"Ah, yes." He reached into his pocket and produced the locket. "I was hoping you'd forgotten."

"I'm sure you were." She seized the locket and placed the new scroll inside before turning her attention back to the scruffy meat suit. "What about him? When you leave him to hijack my body, what's to stop him hurting my friends?"

The demon chuckled. "There's nothing left of him. He is but a shell. Once I am gone, he will die. More's the pity. He could have been useful. Ah, well. Let's get on with it. Did you bring the dagger?"

Reaching behind the band of her jeans, she produced the weapon. For a moment, she considered driving it into his chest, but reconsidered. He'd warned her what he'd do to Susie and her baby if she tried to back out of her agreement. Told her in graphic detail. There was no escaping her fate. She had to obey him or risk the lives of people who had shown her kindness.

She held out the dagger with both hands. "What do you want me to do with it?"

"I only need a little blood." He told her breathlessly, making the hairs on her neck stand at attention. He couldn't hide his excitement. She wondered if her own expression mirrored her feelings of revulsion as he leaned closer. "Just a nick at the wrist will be sufficient. When I merge with your blood, I will enter every organ in your body." Pinching her chin between his finger and thumb, he forced her to face him. "Don't fret, it will all be over soon."

With no other choice, she raised the dagger and drew the blade across her wrist. Blood immediately trickled from the wound and the demon's eyes widened as he licked his lips.

"Good girl."

The meatsuit closed its eyes and dropped to the floor as Evangeline felt the demon enter her body. Pain surged through her, driving her to her knees as she fought his control. Their spirits clashed in a power struggle while she waited for the exact moment to strike. Blood dripped onto the medallion as she held it beneath her open wrist. The seal snapped shut. Binding the contract inside. Forcing the demon to keep his end of the bargain.

"Stop fighting me." He screamed inside her head. "I am part of you now. You cannot drive me from your blood."

"Wanna bet?"

With a quick, accurate sweep of the blade, she sliced from wrist to elbow on her left hand before swapping the dagger to her other hand to repeat the action. Blood pooled by her sides as the demon roared. "What have you done? Fool. You have killed yourself for nothing. I will return in another form once you have bled out."

****

"No, you won't." Christoff caught Evangeline as she slumped to the sand, kneeling beside her. "Will you let me help you, min dyrebare?"

She stared up at him through hooded eyes and smiled. "It's over, Chris. I had to stop him from hurting anyone else through me. I only wish I could have destroyed him altogether."

"It's not over." He lifted her, holding her tight against his chest. "There is a way to defeat him, but it comes at a cost."

"Anything. I'll do anything to stop him."

Tilting her head to the side, he tenderly kissed her throat, briefly savoring the sweet perfume of her skin before sinking his fangs into her carotid artery. Instantly, he felt the power struggle as he drew the demon into his own body. The woman in his arms flailed a little before going limp. He prayed she would survive the experience. Without her, life as he knew it would end.

As the demon merged with his blood, it encountered another foe. One that had resided in Christoff's blood since the day he first became a vampire. A demon as old as time, who did not take kindly to sharing its host with another.

Christoff fell backwards on the sand, still cradling Evangeline in his arms as he fought to hold her demon at bay. The pain cut through him like a knife as the demons battled, each wanting to control his body. When the latest intruder surrendered and tried to flee, he was forced to endure the wrath of both. No way could he let it loose, not until—

"We're here."

He opened his eyes and sighed as David and his family formed a circle around him and his love. As they joined hands, Anna nodded. Her sign to release the demon did not go unnoticed. With a roar, he expelled the demon from his blood. A dark cloud hovered over their heads. Christoff ignored it, leaving Anna to deal with the demon. Evangeline's heart fluttered its last beat as he gnawed a gash in his wrist and held it to her mouth. The blood trickled down her chin, but she did not appear to drink. Overly cautious, he'd taken care to ensure there was no trace of the demon in her blood before attempting to turn her. A vampire with her power and a demon soul would have been disastrous. Had he waited too long? Was it too late?

The sounds of thunder drowned out Anna's chant. Lightning forked through the night sky and rain began to fall as the demon showered their heads with sparks of electricity. Christoff covered Evangeline with his body when Anna's voice rose in volume and her body glowed with ethereal light. Pressure around them built, the mass above them pulsed and deepened in color.

Beneath him, something stirred. A soft groan

spoke volumes to his heart. Evangeline.

"Help me up." As she rose with his assistance, she took the medallion from her pocket, skimmed some of the blood from her wrist and smeared it over the embossed locket. It sprung open in her hand. "Are you ready?"

Anna nodded in response to her question, although her focus remained on the object floating above their heads.

"Let my blood seal your fate."

A gust of wind drew what was left of the demon into the locket. As it snapped shut, Anna clamped her hand down over Evangeline's. A blinding red light burst from between their fingers as their combined power permanently sealed the locket.

"Is it over?" She gazed up into his eyes, expecting an answer. He had none. He asked the same question of Anna.

"Yes. It's over." She smiled, turning her attention back to Evangeline who was placing the medallion into her pocket. "I think I have something else that belongs to you."

They gripped forearms, sparks flying as something mystical seem to pass between them. Even the Corels appeared to be surprised by the phenomenon.

"Phew. I don't know whether to be relieved or depressed about giving that back. I've never felt anything like that. You're more powerful than I ever imagined." Anna leaned against her husband for support. "Thanks for the loan."

****

"It's me who should be doing the thanking." Evangeline told her. "If it wasn't for you, all of you, I'd be dead." She gazed at the faces of her saviors. Every one of them had risked their necks to save her.

Anna gave her the warmest of smiles. "It's the

least we could do. Susie and the baby are precious to us. You gave your life for them. There's no greater sacrifice."

"Holy shit." Evangeline's hand shot to her mouth. "So, I really am dead?"

"Technically, you're undead." Meaghan informed her. "It takes a while to get used to it."

"I think I need a drink." She slipped her fingers between Christoff's and squeezed, grateful for the opportunity to do so.

"Umm. What about this fellow?" David tilted his head in the direction of the discarded body on the beach. "Should we let the sharks have him?"

"Let me clean up my own mess." Evangeline pointed her free hand at the man who had blackened her eye at the library. The man whose soul was as black as the night's sky. With a flick of her wrist, she set his body alight. Within seconds, not even a speck of ash remained.

"Geez. Remind me never to upset her." Derrick told his wife as they all headed towards the house.

Chapter Ten

So, this is what it feels like to be part of a family. Evangeline glanced at the sea of smiling faces as Susie and Terry were ushered into the living area. Once in their seats, Susie sprang to life.

"Okay, spill. No one's told me anything except that the demon is back in the medallion, buried under six feet of concrete in the garden. I want to know every detail of what happened once you left the restaurant yesterday. Don't leave anything out."

Once she had the nod of approval from the others, Evangeline explained what had happened.

"At the restaurant, the demon contacted me telepathically. It said that if I didn't willingly sacrifice myself, it would…" The thought suddenly occurred to her. Should she tell Susie?

"Kill you and the baby." Christoff blurted.

"Nice one, Chris."

"Well, it's the truth." He shrugged. "I'll never understand why you all tiptoe around the facts."

Susie's face paled and she leaned back in Terry's arms. "I don't know how to thank you."

"Don't worry about it." Evangeline felt a tug at her heart strings. What if her plan hadn't worked? What if Susie and the baby had been hurt?

"I still don't understand how you outsmarted the demon," Terry interrupted. "You thought he'd gone before and he came back."

"I had help," she shot Anna a wink, "from a witch and a little black book."

"But—"

"Perhaps it's best you let her tell the story without interruptions."

That's my man. "When I was researching the locket at the library, I found a book about witchcraft and sorcery. It mentioned that power could be shared and that covens do it all the time to intensify their magic. When I realised that I had no choice but to surrender to the demon, I contacted Anna."

"Through a telepathic link?" Susie squealed.

Evangeline laughed. "No, I used the mobile phone that David gave me. Anyway, after picking Chris's pocket and borrowing his car, I met up with Anna in a secluded area and transferred most of my power to her, keeping just enough to hold him off until she could get to me."

"You took a big risk," Chris told her, his expression as serious as the grave. "If Anna hadn't called me, you'd have died before she arrived."

"I did die." She reminded him with a smile. "I died in your arms. I can't think of a better way to end my life."

"Our life is just beginning, min dyrebare." He rose and pulled her up to her feet. "Come, there is something I wish to show you."

They made their excuses and exited the house by the back door. A full moon illuminated the garden and a warm breeze filled the air with the fragrance of frangipani.

"This garden is gorgeous." She breathed in the sweet perfume as she bent down to pick up a stray flower, placing it behind her right ear. He shook his head, took the flower from her hair and placed it behind the left ear.

"This side tells men that you are unavailable. We can't have anyone thinking that you belong to anyone but me."

She wanted to tell him that she was her own woman, that she belonged to no one, but she couldn't lie, even to herself. Lowering her eyes, she asked. "What is it you wanted to show me?"

"Just a little further."

He led her by the hand, down the stairs to the beach and along the sand. Her breath hitched as she passed the patch of sand where her life had ended. Where was he taking her? She hadn't ventured past the rocks before, having been told that this was the border of the Corel property. Had she become a bad influence on Chris? Was he planning to trespass on private property? A shiver of excitement shook her body. Did he propose to skinny dip on a private beach? The thought made her legs weak and her panties damp with desire. She'd unbuttoned the front of her shirt before he'd even noticed and had stripped down to her underwear. As he turned to her, his gaze drifted over her lacy bra and the plump skin spilling over the top.

"You're making this hard for me," he groaned as he cupped her almost bare buttocks and pulled her in for a kiss.

"I sure am." She grinned, stroking the bulge in his jeans. "Do you plan on ravaging me on a private beach? If so, I'm up for the challenge." Tugging at his waistband, she unzipped his fly and slipped her fingers inside the flap of his satin boxers. "What do you think the owner will do if they catch us?"

"Let's find out."

****

He reached down and lifted her, wrapping her long, silky soft legs around his waist, holding her with his left hand while his right unfastened her bra. The dampness of her arousal against his belly sent another rush of blood to his cock. At this rate, they'd never make it to the house.

"Hold on."

He clamped his lips over her nipple, nipping the little bud between his teeth as he transported them inside the home. She closed her eyes and groaned her approval as she forced her breast against his face. By the time she'd opened her eyes, they were in the dining room. Her eyes sparkled with mischief when he lay her down on the edge of the large wooden table and removed her panties.

"Naughty boy." Her hooded eyes beckoned to him. Taunted him. He placed his hands inside her knees and spread her legs wide before him. When he palmed the silken triangle of hair, thumbing the sensitive, swollen bud, she arched her back and moaned her approval. "Fuck the owners. I want you inside me, now."

He didn't hesitate, nor did he remove his clothes. The heady fragrance of her arousal called to him like an aphrodisiac. When she opened her arms, her beautiful flushed breasts heaving, her nipples stiff and pink with desire, his carefully laid plans went out the window. With a thrust, he entered her, groaning as her body wrapped him in a velvet glove of tight heat. With every push, her thighs tightened around his waist, her body held his cock in a vice-like grip as she screamed his name. Sweat trickled between her breasts and he lapped hungrily at the salty goodness, making a mental note to taste more of her later. As her moans overlapped and his own body began to quiver, he dug his fingers into the soft flesh of her buttocks, anchoring himself as she thrust her hips upwards. Her plump breasts bounced against his face as he tried, unsuccessfully, to grip her nipples between his teeth. His extended fangs scraped the skin of her areola and she reacted with an enthusiastic yelp, climaxing so violently, she shook the table. He came in a rush, his body collapsing against her with a final shudder.

"Wow," she whispered in his ear. Her soft breath sending a shiver of desire down his body. "I'd never have expected something so daring from you. Not that I'm complaining, but don't you think we should leave?"

"This was a delicious appetizer," he mumbled against her breast, "but we haven't had the main course."

Hands shoved at his chest. "Seriously. Shouldn't we get going? What do you think the owner would say if he saw us?"

"Well, to use your vernacular, he'd probably say that he wanted to bend you over the couch and fuck your brains out."

When her eyes widened, he couldn't suppress his laughter. She slapped his shoulder and struggled to get off the table. He easily pinned her down.

"I signed the contracts this afternoon. Welcome to your new home."

"You bought this … for me?"

"For us, my darling. I've never bought a home before. If it's not to your liking, we can always purchase another."

She slipped down off the table, her body still flushed and sprinkled with beads of perspiration. Her intoxicating fragrance drove him crazy with desire as she stood naked before him.

"It's beautiful." She turned to him, her eyes brimming with tears. "I wish my mom had lived to see this, see how happy you've made me."

"She shall have pride of place in our garden," he promised. "We will make the arrangements with the funeral home tomorrow."

"How did I ever get so lucky?" she sobbed against his chest. "I don't deserve you."

"Since the moment I first saw you," he lifted her chin, planting a kiss on her forehead, "you put a spell on me."

Her eyes twinkled with mischief and her smile

widened as she told him. "And now you're mine."

The End

www.annieharlandcreek.com

ANNIE HARLAND CREEK

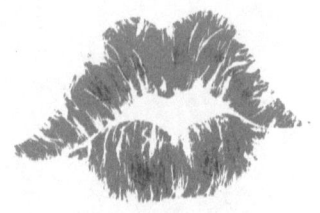

EVERNIGHT PUBLISHING ®

www.evernightpublishing.com